THE BOY AVIA̶ RD
FLI
THE RIVAL AEROPLANE

WILBUR LAWTON

CHAPTER I. THE BIG PRIZE.

"Phew!" exclaimed Billy Barnes as he reported for work on the New York *Planet* one broiling afternoon in late August, "this is a scorcher and no mistake."

"I should think after all your marvelous adventures with the Boy Aviators that you would be so used to heat and cold and hardship that you wouldn't kick at a little thing like a warm day."

The remark came from a young fellow about twenty-one years old who occupied a desk beside that of the stout spectacled youth of eighteen whom our readers have already met as Billy Barnes.

"Why, hullo, Fred Reade!" said Billy, looking up with a good-natured grin from the operation of opening his typewriter desk, "I thought you were off covering aviation."

"I was," rejoined the other, with a near approach to a sneer, "but since we printed your story about the recovery of the treasure on the Spanish galleon I guess they think I'm not good enough to cover the subject."

If the good-natured Billy Barnes noticed the close approach to outspoken enmity with which these words were spoken he gave no sign of it. Any reply he might have made was in fact cut short at that minute by an office boy who approached him.

"Mr. Stowe wants to see you, Mr. Barnes, at once, please," said the lad.

"There you go, the managing editor sending for you as soon as you get back. I wish I was a pet," sneered Reade as Billy hastened after the boy and the next minute entered a room screened off from the editorial department by a glass door bearing the words "Managing Editor."

At a desk above which hung "This is my busy day," and other signs not calculated to urge visitors to become conversational, sat a heavy-set, clean-shaven man with a big pair of spectacles astride his nose. He had a fat cigar in his mouth which he regarded as he spoke with far more intensity than he did Billy.

"Afternoon, Barnes," was his greeting.

"Good afternoon, Mr. Stowe," returned the young reporter, "you sent for me— —"

"Sit down," said the other brusquely, indicating a chair.

Billy sat down and waited for the next words of his managing editor.

"The *Planet*, as you know, has made a specialty of featuring aviation," continued Mr. Stowe, gazing fixedly at his cigar.

Billy nodded, the remark did not seem to call for a more definite reply.

"We have offered prizes for flights from time to time, and in this way have obtained a reputation as an authority on aviation and a patron of what is bound to be the vehicle of the coming ages."

Again Billy nodded at the managing editor's rather florid way of putting it.

"For instance, the $10,000 Albany-New York flight and the $30,000 New York-St. Louis flight. The $100,000 offer for a transatlantic flight as yet remains unchallenged for, but I have no doubt that in time some daring aviator will make the attempt."

"It should be possible," once more agreed Billy, wondering what was coming next.

"In the meantime," Mr. Stowe continued, "the *Despatch* has declared itself our rival in this field by also devoting great attention to the subject, and offering prizes for flights in opposition to our original idea. The owner of the *Planet* has therefore decided to eclipse all previous offers and be the first in the field with a prize of $50,000 for a flight from New York to San Francisco, or as far in that direction as possible. The air craft that travels furthest will get the prize."

"Across the continent?" gasped Billy.

"Exactly. We are going to publish the conditions and date of starting in our to-morrow morning's issue. And the offer incidentally means a great chance for you."

Billy gave a questioning glance.

"I intend to have you follow the racers in an automobile and send dispatches from the various points along the route concerning the progress of the cross-country aerial racers."

The young reporter's face beamed.

"That's mighty good of you, sir," he said earnestly.

"Not at all. It's simply the selection of the best man for the job; that's all. You have far more knowledge of aviation than Reade—or at least you ought to have after your long association with the Boy Aviators—and therefore we have selected you."

"As to the conditions of the race, Mr. Stowe—how about stops, gasolene and water stations, and so on?"

"Each contestant will be expected to arrange those details for himself," was the answer. "This newspaper simply offers the prize to the first aeroplane to arrive in San Francisco, or go furthest in that direction. Also, of course, we claim the privilege of getting exclusive accounts of the doings of the *Planet* aeroplanes. That's all. Simple, isn't it?"

"Very," agreed Billy as he took his leave. "By the way, sir, does any one else know of your offer?"

"Nobody; not even Reade. I guess he's pretty sore that we took him off aviation on the eve of making the prize offer, but it can't be helped."

"Why, I—you see, sir, I'd rather not take it, if it is blocking Reade in any way. I don't want to take the assignment at all if it's going to hurt Reade with the paper."

The managing editor gave an impatient wave of his hand.

"Let me attend to Reade," he remarked impatiently, "you go and get out a story for to-morrow about possible contestants. Of course your friends, the Chester boys, will enter?"

Billy looked dubious.

"I don't know," he replied. "I rather think they were planning for a rest and to continue their studies, and this cross-country flight won't be any picnic. However, I hope they do enter," replied Billy.

"I had no idea that there would be any doubt about it," said Mr. Stowe impatiently, "well, do the best you can. Anyhow, get interviews with Blewitt, Sharkness and Auldwin. They will be sure to enter their machines, and let's have a good, live story for to-morrow. By the way, not a word of this to anybody but the aviators you may see till we publish the offer. The *Despatch* would be quite capable of offering a similar prize to-morrow morning if they learned what was in the wind."

Billy nodded as Mr. Stowe once more gave a sign of dismissal, and hastened from the room. So hurried was his exit, in fact, that he almost bumped into Reade as he made his way out. The editorial room was deserted, except for the dark-haired, slender young fellow with whom Billy had almost collided. The other reporters were all out on their assignments.

"Well?" were Fred Reade's first words.

"Well," rejoined Billy, adjusting his spectacles, which had narrowly escaped being jarred off his nose in the bump, "isn't there room enough in the place without your getting so near that door that you almost upset my slender form?"

"Never mind that," replied Frank Reade; "what I want to know is, how do I stand in there?"

He motioned with his head toward the managing editor's room from which the boys were by this time several paces removed.

"I don't understand you exactly," was Billy's reply. He noticed that Reade's face bore an angry flush and he seemed excited.

"What I mean is this: Am I going to continue to do aviation for the *Planet*?"

"Say, Fred, old man, I'm awfully sorry — —"

"Oh, cut that out. You don't mean it, and you know you don't. You wanted to grab off the job for yourself, and I can see by your face that you have."

"If you mean that I am to do aviation for the *Planet* in future, you are right," replied Billy. "I am; but it was only on Mr. Stowe's orders. You're wrong, Fred, and you know you are, when you accuse me of trying to take your job away from you."

"Oh, rot," exclaimed the other angrily. "If that had been the case you'd have kept away. You don't have to work. You made plenty of money out of your share of the Golden Galleon treasure. You have just deliberately tried to oust me from my job."

"You talk as if you'd been fired," said Billy. "You know that you are one of the most valued reporters on the *Planet*."

"Don't try to jolly me," rejoined the other angrily. "And as for being fired, I don't have to be, for I've got my resignation ready written out. Here copy boy!" he cried, "take this note in to Mr. Stowe."

As the boy hurried up Reade drew from his pocket an envelope and handed it to the lad.

"Hold on there!" cried Billy, genuinely moved at Reade's evident chagrin, "have you gone crazy, Fred? What's the matter?"

"Take that note in," thundered Reade to the hesitating boy, who thereupon hurried off, "it's your fault I've had to quit, Billy Barnes, and I'll not forget it, I can promise you. I'll get even with you for this in a way you don't suspect. No; I won't shake hands with you. I don't want to speak to you."

Reade flung angrily off and put on his coat and hat. Without taking any more notice of Billy he strode out of the *Planet* offices and into the street.

On the sidewalk he paused for a minute. His hat shoved back off his brow and his forehead puckered in perplexity.

"I'll do it," he exclaimed suddenly under his breath as if he had made up his mind to something. "I'll do it. The *Despatch* will jump at it, and I'll get even on Billy Barnes and the *Planet* at the same time."

CHAPTER II. BILLY AS A DIPLOMAT.

A few minutes after Fred Reade had left the *Planet* offices he was followed by Billy Barnes. The young reporter boarded an open Madison Avenue car, preferring it to the stuffy heat of the subway, and in due time found himself at the home of Mr. Chester, the wealthy banker, and father of Frank and Harry Chester, the Boy Aviators. The lads need no further introduction to our readers, who have doubtless formed the acquaintance of both the young air pilots in previous volumes of this series. To those who have not it may be as well—while Billy Barnes is ringing the doorbell—to say that Frank and Harry Chester were graduates of the Agassiz High School and the pioneers among schoolboy aviators. Beginning with models of air craft they had finally evolved a fine biplane which they named the *Golden Eagle*. The first *Golden Eagle* was destroyed in a tropical storm off the coast of Nicaragua, as related in The Boy Aviators in Nicaragua; or, In League with the Insurgents. To carry out an important commission affecting a stolen formula the lads then constructed a second *Golden Eagle*, in which they met many adventures and perils in the Everglades of Florida. These were set forth in The Boy Aviators on Secret Service; or, Working with Wireless, the second volume of the series. In the third and fourth volumes the boys had aerial adventures in Africa, and in the Sargasso Sea. What these were will be found in The Boy Aviators in Africa; or, An Aerial Ivory Trail; and The Boy Aviators' Treasure Quest; or, The Golden Galleon.

Before the servant who answered Billy's ring had time to announce him there was a rush of feet down the hallway and two tall lads, with crisp wavy hair and blue eyes, were wringing Billy's hand till he laughingly shouted:

"Hey, let up! I'm not the India-rubber man with the circus."

At this moment a door opened and a gray-haired man stepped out. It was Mr. Chester.

"Why, how do you do, Billy Barnes," he exclaimed heartily, "glad to see you; but I hope you haven't come to take my boys off again on some wonderful trip or other. You know their mother and I like to see them at home sometimes."

8

"Well, sir," began Billy somewhat abashed, "the fact is I—you see—I mean—well, the long and short of it is, sir, that I *have* an adventurous proposal to make to them."

"Hurray!" shouted Harry. "Good for you, Billy!"

Mr. Chester, however, assumed his—what Frank called—"official face."

"Really, I— —" he began.

"Now, father," interjected Frank, "don't you think it would be a good idea if we heard what Billy's proposal, or whatever you like to call it, is before we say anything more?"

"Perhaps you are right, my boy," said his father, "but I am busy now, and— —"

"We'll take Billy out to the workshop and make him tell us all about it, and then we'll submit it to you," suggested Harry.

"That's a good idea," assented his father.

Five minutes later the three boys were closeted in the big room above the garage of the Chester home, which served them as a workshop, study and designing plant all rolled into one. The blue prints, aeroplane parts, chemicals, and tools scattered about or ranged in neat racks against the walls in conjunction with a shelf of books on aviation and kindred subjects, the table illumined by movable drop lights shaded by green shades, gave the room a very business-like appearance. It was clearly a place for work and not for play—as a sort of framework newly erected in one corner showed.

"What's that?" asked Billy, indicating it.

"Oh, just an idea we were working on for a wireless adapted for auto use," rejoined Frank, "but never mind that now. What's this wonderful plan of yours?"

"Simply this," replied Billy briskly, "how'd you fellows like to get $50,000?"

"Would we?" exclaimed Harry. "Lead us to it."

"You'll have to lead yourselves," laughed Billy.

"Oh, come on, Billy, put us out of our suspense. What do you mean?" said Frank.

"Well, my paper, *The Planet*, you know," began Billy, "has decided to offer the amount I named for a successful flight from here to San Francisco, or as near to that city as can be attained. There are no conditions—except get there first, or travel furthest."

"Well?" said Frank.

"Well," repeated Billy, "I've come here to interview you. Are you ready to announce yourselves as competitors for the *Planet's* contest?"

Not so much to Billy's surprise Frank shook his head.

"I don't know what to say," he rejoined. "It isn't a thing you can make your mind up to in a minute. I'd like to do it, but it would require a lot of preparation. Then, too, there would be maps to get up and a thousand and one details to arrange. It's a big task—bigger than you imagine, Billy."

"Oh, I know it's a big proposition," said the young reporter, "that's one reason I thought it would appeal to you," he added subtly. "As for gasolene, why not carry a supply of it in the automobile?"

"What automobile?" asked Harry.

"Why, didn't I tell you," exclaimed Billy, "the auto I'm to follow you fellows in and send out accounts of your progress. Oh, Frank, please say you'll do it—it would be bully."

"It would be bully, no doubt of that," rejoined Frank; "but I have a lot of experimental work on hand that I want to finish. I should have to leave that, and Harry is preparing for college. No, Billy, I'm afraid we shall have to call it off. There are lots of other aviators you can get to take part. The prize is big enough to call out the biggest of them."

Bitter disappointment showed on Billy's face.

"Then it's all off?" he murmured dejectedly.

"I'm afraid so—yes," replied Frank. "What do you say, Harry?"

"I'd like to go," decided Harry promptly; "but, as you said, Frank, it would delay us both in our studies, and then we would have a lot of work to do on the framework of the *Golden Eagle*, wrecked as she was."

"Hold on there!" cried Billy. "I was coming to that. I was going to say that maybe the reason you refused was that you couldn't build a new 'plane in time, but did I understand you to say you had recovered the frame?"

"Of the old *Golden Eagle II*," put in Frank. "You recollect that following the fight with Luther Barr's dirigible in the Sargasso we had to abandon her."

"After that rascal Sanborn tried to blow a hole in the pontoons that made her float and sink her."

"I shall never forget the look on his face as that devil fish seized him and bore him to the depths of the sea," shuddered Harry.

"Nor I," said Frank; "but here's your story, Billy. Having, as you know, left the *Golden Eagle* drifting on her pontoons we never thought we should see her again, but a few days ago a message reached us from Florida saying that the government derelict destroyer *Grampus*, while on the lookout for dangerous wrecks in the Caribbean Sea, encountered a strange-looking object scudding over—or rather through—the waves. They set out in chase and soon made it out as the framework of an aeroplane. You remember that I advertised the loss of our air craft pretty extensively in marine and naval journals, and offered a reward, so that when the drifting aeroplane was sighted every man on board the government vessel was eager to capture it. As the wind dropped soon after they sighted it they were enabled to get alongside the derelict and found that it was indeed the

Golden Eagle. Her planes were riddled with bullets and her pontoons covered with green seaweed, but the framework was as solid and the braces as taut as the day we put her together. Moreover, the engine, beyond being badly coated with rust, was as good as the day we set it on the bed plate."

"Say, why didn't you tell me about this before?" demanded Billy.

"Too much of a hurry to get her back, I guess," rejoined Frank. "But, say," he broke off, "the frame was shipped from Florida and arrived here this morning. Want to look at it?"

"Want to look at it? You bet I do!" gasped Billy. "That's the finest old air ship in the world."

"So we think," laughed Harry, as Frank led the way down a flight of steps into the garage below the room in which they had been discussing the *Planet's* offer.

Frank switched on the lights and there stood revealed in the rear of the place a shadowy framework that glistened in places where the light caught it. It towered huge, and yet light and airy-looking, like the skeleton of a strange bird.

"It wasn't shipped that way?" asked Billy.

"Not much," was Frank's reply. "They took it down in Florida and boxed it."

"And a nice mess they made of it," said Harry; "but, thank goodness, they didn't harm the engine."

He pointed to the motor which was out of the machine and lay in a corner.

"Doesn't look very big for the work it's done, does it?" laughed Frank, gazing lovingly at the eight-cylindered, hundred horse-power engine that had performed such good service since the boys installed it.

"There's certainly a lot of cleaning to be done about the 'plane," remarked Billy, as he handled the rusted frames and tarnished bronze parts.

"Oh, that won't take long," replied Frank lightly; "anyhow, we've got lots of time to do it."

"Unless," put in Billy.

"Well, unless what?" demanded Frank, though he guessed the young reporter's meaning.

"Unless you go in for that $50,000 prize," cried Billy skillfully evading the playful blow Frank aimed at him. "In all seriousness, Frank, won't you?" he pleaded.

"In all seriousness, no," was Frank's rejoinder. "I'd like to do it. Billy," he went on. "I'd like to do it for your sake, if it would do you any good — we both would, wouldn't we, Harry?"

"You bet," replied the younger brother with effective brevity.

"Well, of course, I know you fellows too well to try to urge you," said Billy; "but I would like to be able to announce in the *Planet* to-morrow that the Boy Aviators announce they will compete for the paper's big prize."

"To tell you the truth, Billy," laughed Frank, "we've had about enough newspaper notoriety lately. It's mighty good of you to write accounts of our adventures, but I guess the papers can get along for a while without anything about us."

"Not at all, you make good copy," declared Billy, with such comic emphasis that the boys went off into shouts of laughter.

And so it came about that Billy said good-night without having shaken the Boy Aviators in their determination not to engage in any public flights, but all the time, though they little knew it, events were so shaping themselves that little as they dreamed it they were to take part in the record flight.

CHAPTER III. UNDER A CLOUD.

It was early the next morning. The paper had been put to bed. Billy, with the satisfied feeling that came to him with the knowledge that he had written a good introduction and account of the *Planet's* great offer, was slipping into his coat preparatory to going home, when Mr. Stowe, his face purple with anger, called to him in a sharp voice from the door of the editorial sanctum.

"Come here, Barnes, I want to see you," he said brusquely.

"Hullo, something's up with the chief," thought Billy to himself; but he answered cheerily: "All right, sir," with an inward feeling that something was all wrong.

"Look here, Barnes," exclaimed Mr. Stowe, angrily flourishing a first edition of the *Planet's* rival, the *Despatch*, "there has been treachery somewhere. How about this?"

Billy, with an unaccountable sinking of the heart, took the paper the other flourished so furiously. It was still moist and warm as it had been run off the press. The sickly, sweet odor of printer's ink hung about it. But these details did not attract Billy's attention. And for an excellent reason. Staring him in the face in big black letters he read:

THE "DESPATCH" OFFERS FIFTY THOUSAND
DOLLARS FOR A TRANSCONTINENTAL
FLIGHT.

Below — and every letter of the article burned itself into Billy's brain, was a long story eulogizing the enterprise of the *Despatch* in making the offer and giving a list of the noted aviators who would be sure — so the *Despatch* thought — to enter the contest.

It was a cold steal of the *Planet's* idea.

Almost word for word the conditions were the same as those Mr. Stowe had detailed to Billy that afternoon.

"Well," remarked the managing editor in a harsh tone, in which Billy recognized the steely ring that always presaged a storm from that august quarter.

"Well," floundered Billy helplessly, "I cannot account for it."

"You cannot," echoed the other in a flinty tone.

"Why no," rejoined the lad, lifting his eyes to Stowe's, "can you?"

"Yes I can."

"You can, sir?"

"We have been sold out."

"Sold out?"

"Precisely. And there are only three people in the office who could have had any knowledge of the secret. One is the owner of the paper, the other myself and the third is you."

Mr. Stowe joined his hands magisterially and looked straight at Billy, in whose mind a horrid suspicion had begun to dawn.

The managing editor was practically accusing him of selling the story.

Preposterous as the idea was, Billy realized that to a prejudiced mind, such as the managing editor's, there would be no way of explaining matters. His thoughts were suddenly broken in on by Mr. Stowe's harsh voice.

"Is there any one else, Barnes?"

Like a flash the recollection of his encounter with Reade at the very door of the managing editor's room, the latter's strange and defiant manner, and the unaccountable publishing by the *Despatch* of a rival offer, came into Billy's mind. He was about to mention Reade's name when he checked himself.

What proof had he?

Then, too, he saw that Stowe's mind was made up. He did not wish to appear in the position of trying to throw the blame on a man whom he realized the managing editor would not believe could by any possibility have any knowledge of the *Planet's* plans.

"I am waiting for your answer," came the cold, incisive voice again.

"I can think of none, sir," rejoined the young reporter with a feeling that he had put the rope about his neck with a vengeance now.

"Hum! In that case, by a process of elimination, we have only one person who could have done it, and that— —" He paused. "I hate to have to say it, Barnes, but it looks bad for you."

"Great Heavens, Mr. Stowe!" gasped Billy, who, while he had seen what the managing editor was leading up to, was struck by a rude shock of surprise at the actual placing into words of the accusation, "do you mean to say you think that I would do such a thing?"

"I don't know what to think, Barnes," was the discouraging answer. "I am more sorry than I can say to have had to speak as I have. However, until you can clear yourself of the cloud of a suspicion that must rest on you because of this affair we shall have to part company."

Billy went white.

His superior then really believed him guilty of the worst crime a newspaper man can commit—a breach of faith to his paper.

"Do you really believe what you are saying, sir?" he demanded.

"As I said before, I don't know what to think, Barnes. However, what I might say will make little difference. In a short time the proprietor will hear of this, and I should have to discharge you whether I wished to or no. If you wish to act now, you may resign."

"Very well, then, Mr. Stowe, I will make out my formal resignation," exclaimed Billy, his cheeks burning crimson with anger and shame.

"I'm sorry, Barnes," said Mr. Stowe, as the lad, scarcely knowing where he was going, left the room. "I have no other course, you know."

Fifteen minutes later Billy Barnes was no longer a member of the *Planet* staff, and his resignation, neatly typewritten, lay on the managing editor's desk. To do Mr. Stowe justice, he had acted against his own beliefs, but he was only an inferior officer in the direction of the paper. Its owner, he well knew, was a man of violent temper and fixed convictions. When he saw the *Despatch* Mr. Stowe knew that the vials of his wrath would be emptied and that Billy would have had to leave in any event. And so subsequent events proved, for the next day, when Billy's immediate discharge was angrily demanded by the *Planet's* owner, he was informed by his managing editor that the boy had left of his own free will.

"He resigned last night rather than have any suspicion directed toward him," said Mr. Stowe; "but, you mark my words, the boy will right himself."

"Nonsense, Stowe, he sold us out," said the owner bitterly; "sold us out cold and nothing will ever make me alter my conviction."

"Except Billy Barnes himself," said Stowe softly, and lit a cigar, which he puffed at with great energy.

When he had learned that Reade was doing aviation for the *Despatch* the managing editor's mind was crossed for a brief minute with suspicion that here might be the traitor. But he dismissed it—was compelled to, in fact. To his mind it would have been an impossibility for Reade to have heard the conversation in which the offer was discussed.

In the meantime both papers continued to work up their $50,000 offers, until there was actually developed a keen and bitter rivalry between them. One morning the *Despatch* would announce the entry of some prominent aviator in its cross-country contest, and the next the *Planet* would be out with its announcement of a new contestant added to its ranks. The public appetite was whetted to a keen pitch by the various moves.

Crawford, the man who had taken Billy Barnes' place on the *Planet*, was a skilled writer, and an excellent man to work up such a story as the cross-continental challenge. It was he who first broached to Stowe the idea of flinging down the gauntlet to the *Despatch* and inviting that paper to start its contestants on the same day as those of the *Planet*, the winner to take the prizes of both papers. This would give the struggle tremendous added interest, and attract worldwide attention, he argued.

While events were thus shaping themselves with the *Planet* and the *Despatch*, Billy Barnes had visited his friends, the Boy Aviators, and told them, with a rueful face, of his misfortune.

His manner of so doing was characteristic. A few days after he had left the newspaper he called on them at their work shop. To his surprise he found there old Eben Joyce, the inventor whom Luther Barr had treated so shabbily in the matter of the *Buzzard* aeroplane of which Joyce was the creator — as told in The Boy Aviators' Treasure Quest; or, The Golden Galleon.

Joyce and the two boys were busied over the *Golden Eagle* when Billy arrived, adjusting a strange-looking mechanism to it, consisting of a boxed flywheel of glittering brass encased in a framework of the same metal. It seemed quite a heavy bit of apparatus, withal so delicately balanced, that it adjusted itself to every movement of its frame. A second glance showed Billy that it was a gyroscope.

The boys and the aged inventor were so deeply interested in examining the bit of machinery that they did not hear Billy come in, and it was not till he hailed them with a cheery:

"Come down from the clouds, you fellows!" that they turned with a shout of recognition.

"Why, hullo, Billy Barnes!" they cried, "what are you after now? If you want an aeroplane story here's a good one — a new adjustable gyroscopic appliance for attachment to aeroplanes which renders them stable in any shifting wind currents."

"It's a jim-dandy," enthusiastically cried Harry.

"But it's a story you can't use," added Frank, "because the appliance, which is the invention of Mr. Joyce—has not yet been fully patented. He has been good enough to let us try it out."

"It looks fine," said Billy, who knew about as much about gyroscopes as a cat knows of the solar system; "but you needn't worry about my printing anything about it, Frank. You see, I'm fired," he added simply.

"Fired?" cried Frank.

"Well, about the same thing—I resigned, as a matter of fact," explained Billy ruefully; "but it all amounts to the same in the long run."

"Sit down and tell us about it," commanded Frank, genuinely concerned at his friend's evident dejection.

Seated on an upturned box, which had contained batteries, Billy related his story, omitting nothing. On his suspicions of Reade, however, he touched lightly.

"You see, I've got nothing on the fellow," he explained, "and although I'm convinced that he gave our plan away to the *Despatch*, yet I've got nothing to base it on."

"That's so," Frank and Harry were compelled to admit.

The three friends spent an hour or so chatting, and then Mr. Joyce, who had been tinkering with his aeroplane attachment quite oblivious to their talk, announced that he would have to be going home. He had some work to do on another invention that evening, he explained.

"Well, say, as we've been stuffing in here almost all day and it's warm enough to be mighty uncomfortable, what do you say if we take a little spin out in the auto. We can give Mr. Joyce a ride home," exclaimed Frank.

"The very thing," agreed Harry.

Old Mr. Joyce was nothing loath to be spared the long ride in a train to his home in the outskirts of Jersey City. As for Billy Barnes, he was delighted at the idea.

Accordingly, half an hour later the Chester boys' auto rolled on board one of the ferryboats which ply across the North River to Jersey City. The boat had hardly reached midstream before they were aware of another car almost opposite to them in the space set apart for autos in the centre of the boat. Before five minutes had passed they also noticed that they were the object of close scrutiny on the part of one of the occupants of the machine. He was a tall youth with dark hair and eyes, and as soon as he observed that he was attracting their attention he at once withdrew his gaze.

Billy Barnes, who had been "stretching his legs" by a stroll on the stern deck of the ferryboat as she made her way across the river, rejoined the others just as the boat was pulling into her slip.

"Hullo!" he exclaimed as the autos rolled over the apron and onto the wharf, "there's Fred Reade."

He indicated the occupant of the other car, who seemed to have taken so much interest in the Chester boys and Eben Joyce, their aged companion.

CHAPTER IV. THIEVES IN THE NIGHT.

The other occupants of the auto were a man with a heavy red beard and a nervous, alert little man whom Billy said was an aviator named Slade.

"That's queer to see Reade over here. I wonder what he can be doing," said Billy, as the two autos left the shed and emerged into the street.

Neither of the boys could, of course, hazard a guess, but had they known it the mission of the reporter who had betrayed the *Planet* was more nearly concerned with them than they imagined. The car in which Reade was seated seemed a more powerful machine than the one the boys occupied and it soon left them behind. They thought no more of the chance encounter and soon arrived at the home of Eben Joyce, a comfortable cottage on the heights overlooking the "meadows" on one side and the North river on the other.

They were greeted by the inventor's daughter, who seemed much disturbed.

"Oh, I am so glad you have come!" she exclaimed, after she had invited the little party in.

"Why, what has happened?" asked Frank.

"I will tell you," she said, while they all leaned forward deeply interested. "This afternoon I was called to the door by a man in ragged clothes who begged me for something to eat. My father has told me never to let anyone go away hungry, so I told the servant to give the man some food. I thought no more of the matter till, on looking out of the window, I saw the man who had asked for charity going toward the old barn out there that my father used as a workshop."

Old Mr. Joyce became greatly excited. It was evident he feared some harm had come to his collection of scientific instruments and plans for inventions which he housed there for lack of room in the house.

"Yes, yes, go on," he exclaimed, quivering with agitation.

"He was fumbling with the lock when I looked up and saw him. I shouted to him to know what he was doing. His reply was to instantly stop what he was at and run toward the front of the house. I opened the door just in time to see him leap into an automobile in which were two other men, and they drove off."

"A tramp in an automobile; that's funny," commented Frank.

"Indeed it is. In fact, I recollect thinking at the time that he asked me for food that his manner was too refined to be that of a genuine tramp."

"What did he look like?" asked Harry.

"He was tall and had a big red beard. That is all I am able to recollect of him."

"Sounds like the man we saw in Reade's auto," exclaimed Harry.

"Can Fred Reade have anything to do with this mysterious happening?" asked Billy.

"Eh, say that name again, young man," demanded the inventor, who was, besides being often preoccupied, somewhat deaf and so had not heard Billy mention the other's name when they were in the auto.

"I said Fred Reade," rejoined Billy. "Why, do you know him?"

"I do, and I know no good of him," was the reply. "It was he that first approached me in connection with the sale of the *Buzzard* to Luther Barr and — —"

"Luther Barr again. We seem to cross his trail all the time," exclaimed Frank.

"Eh?" questioned the old man, his hand at his ear, trumpet-wise.

"I said we have heard of Luther Barr before, as you know," said Frank, "but you never mentioned the fact that Reade had acted for him."

"It must have slipped my mind in the excitement," explained the old man. "Yes, Fred Reade has acted for Barr in many matters that I know of."

"A sort of agent of his," said Billy.

"More than that," rejoined old Eben Joyce; "there is some mysterious tie between them. I think Reade knows something about Luther Barr that the other is afraid will come out."

"How is that?" asked Frank.

"I don't know, but such is my impression. At the time of the negotiation for the *Buzzard* Reade treated Barr as an equal more than if he were employed by him."

It had grown dusk by this time and Eben Joyce's daughter lit the lamp and set it down on the cottage table. As she did so there came a loud roar of an approaching motor car down the quiet street and the next moment through the gathering gloom a big auto approached the cottage. As it neared it it slowed down. They all went out on the porch to see who could be driving a car down that little frequented street. It was not very light, but as the car drew nearer Frank recognized it.

"That's Fred Reade's auto," he cried.

But if the boys imagined that they were to get any solution of the car's mysterious appearance they were mistaken. As it neared the house, and the group on the porch must have been plainly visible to its occupants, the big car suddenly leaped forward and shot away into the darkness.

"What did they do that for?" asked Billy.

"I guess they saw so many if us here that they thought it would be more prudent to stay away," suggested Frank.

"What can they be after?" wondered Harry.

"The blue prints of my gyroscopic attachment and possibly my experimental machine itself," declared the inventor, "though if they had the blue prints they could easily manufacture them themselves. Reade has been after me to sell them."

"That is so," mused Frank; "undoubtedly such prints would be of great value to them."

"Will you do something for me?" inquired old Eben Joyce, suddenly.

"Of course," rejoined Frank; "what is it?"

"Will you take charge of my blue prints for me. It is lonely here and I am old and my daughter unprotected. In case they attacked us in the night we should have little opportunity to keep the prints from them. I would feel quite secure if you had them in your possession, however."

Frank readily agreed to this, adding that he would place them in a safe deposit vault.

"I shall rest much easier if you would," said the old inventor. "Bad as they are, I don't think the men would hurt us; all they are after is the plans and I really dare not have them about here another night."

It was an hour later when, with the plans safely tucked away in an inside pocket of Frank's coat, the boys started back for town.

"If you feel at all nervous we will telephone home and stay here with you," Frank offered before they left.

"Oh, not at all," exclaimed old Joyce, who was already busy figuring a new problem. "I have a revolver and I will communicate with the police about my fears. I shall be all right."

With hearty good nights the boys' car swung off, its headlights glowing brightly. They sped along through the outskirts of Jersey City and were about to leave the lonely, badly-lighted section through which they had been passing when suddenly a figure stepped full into the path of light cast ahead of them.

The sudden apparition of the night was waving a red lantern.

"Stop! there's danger ahead!" it shouted.

"Danger, what sort of danger?" asked Frank, nevertheless bringing the car to a stop.

"Why, there's an excavation ahead. Ah! that's right, you've stopped. Now then, young gentlemen, just step out of the petroleum phaeton and fork over the contents of your pockets."

"What, you rascal, are you holding us up?" cried Billy indignantly, as the man pointed a revolver at them.

"Looks that way, doesn't it?" grinned the other. "Come on now, shell out and hurry up."

As he spoke three other figures glided from the shadows of an untenanted house near by and silently took up their positions a short distance beyond him. They were out of the path of the auto's lights and their faces could not be seen. The light glinted on something that each held in his hand, however, and which were clearly enough revolvers. Things looked pretty blue for the Boy Aviators.

The sudden turn events had taken almost bereft Frank of his wits for a minute, but suddenly it flashed across him that the man who had waved the lantern did not talk like an ordinary robber and that it was remarkable that the others took so much trouble to keep out of the light. The next instant his suspicions were confirmed by hearing the voice of the first comer snap out:

"Which one of you has got them gyroscope plans?"

Frank's reply was startling. Without uttering a word he suddenly drove the machine full speed ahead.

It leaped forward like a frightened wild thing.

As it dashed ahead it bowled over the would-be robber, but that he was not seriously hurt the boys judged by the volley of bad language he sent after them. As for the others, as the car made its leap they had stepped nimbly aside.

"Look out for the excavation. Frank; we'll be in it!" shouted Billy in an alarmed voice as the car rushed forward.

"Why, there's no excavation, Billy," rejoined Frank, bending over the steering wheel. "That was just a bluff on the part of those men, of whom, if I am not much mistaken, Fred Reade was one."

CHAPTER V. THE BOYS DECIDE.

Their strange experience of the preceding night was naturally the topic of the day with the boys the next morning. That Fred Reade was concerned in it there seemed no reason to doubt, though just what part he had played was more shadowy. A perusal of the two newspapers, the *Planet* and the *Despatch*, the next day, however, gave the boys an inkling of one of his motives for his desperate attempt—if, indeed, it had been engineered by him—to gain possession of the Joyce gyroscope. This was the announcement that the two papers had agreed to start their contestants off in a spirit of rivalry by naming the same day for the start and imposing exactly the same conditions, the prizes to be lumped. Among other things in the *Despatch's* article the boys read that Slade, the noted aviator, was an entrant.

"Mr. Reade," the paper stated, "will accompany Mr. Slade as the correspondent of this newspaper. He will ride in an automobile which will carry supplies and emergency tools and equipment. Every step of the trip will be chronicled by him."

There was more to the same effect, but the boys had no eyes for it after their sight lighted on the following paragraph:

"Those remarkable and precocious youths, the Boy Aviators, are, of course, not equipped for such a contest as this, requiring, as it does, an excess of skill and knowledge of aviation. A noted aviator of this city, in speaking of the fact that they have not entered their names, remarked that boys are not calculated to have either the energy or the pluck to carry them through an enterprise like the present."

"That's Fred Reade, for a bet," exclaimed Billy, as he read the insulting paragraph. "He's crazy sore at you and everyone else beside his sweet self. I suppose he wrote that just to make himself disagreeable."

"Moreover, he knows in some mysterious way that we have the first option on the Joyce gyroscope," put in Harry, "and maybe he wouldn't give his eyes to get it for the principal *Planet* contestant."

"He's certainly shown that," said Frank. "I've heard of the Slade machine, and it is reputed to be a wonder. In whatever way Reade heard that we had the gyroscope, there is little doubt that he realizes that fitted with it the Slade plane might win the race."

"And there's another reason," burst out Billy Barnes. "You see now that the two papers have agreed to run the race off together it eliminates the two prizes, and according to the conditions both will be massed and awarded to the winner."

"Well?" questioned Frank.

"Well," repeated Billy, continuing, "this means that if Reade has been backing Slade to win the *Despatch* contest, and there is little doubt he has — now that the two contests are massed if Slade has a better man on the *Planet's* list pitted against him the *Planet* man may win, and then Reade gets nothing."

"You mean that Slade was almost certain to win the *Despatch's* race — that the $50,000 was as good as won with the class of contestants he had against him before the two offers were massed?" asked Frank.

Billy nodded. "And that now, for all they know, the *Planet* may have some dark horse who will beat Slade and get the combined prize?"

"Precisely, as Ben Stubbs would say," laughed Billy.

"It would serve them right for the mean trick they tried to play on us by attempting to steal the gyroscope plans if we were to enter in the race at the last moment and be the *Planet's* dark horses." mused Frank.

"Oh, Frank, do you mean that?" shouted Billy.

"I haven't said I mean anything, you wild man," laughed Frank, "but inasmuch as my father was talking of going to Los Angeles — you know he has some orange groves out there — I've been thinking that we might combine business with pleasure and take a trip to California by aeroplane."

"Then you'll do it," eagerly demanded Billy. As for Harry, he was so entranced at the idea that he was capering about the room like an Indian.

"I think that it is almost certain that we will not," teased Frank.

"Not what?" groaned Billy.

"Not be able to resist the temptation of going."

At this point a maid entered the room with a telegram.

"This is for you," she said, holding it out to Frank.

Frank tore it open and his face flushed angrily as he read its contents. He handed it to the others. The message was not signed, but even so the boys all guessed who it was from.

"You got away from us by a neat trick last night," it read, "but puppies like you cannot balk us. Men are in this race, not boys, so keep your hands off it."

"I suppose he means by that, as we are not contestants, we have no right to interfere with their attempts to steal the gyroscope attachment for themselves," exclaimed Frank. "That's a fine line of reasoning."

"That telegram ought to decide us," burst out Harry.

"It certainly ought to," chimed in Billy.

At that minute the Chester boys' father entered the room.

"What are you boys all so excited about?" he asked.

"What would you say if we joined you in Los Angeles?" asked Frank.

"What do you mean? I don't quite understand," said Mr. Chester, puzzled in spite of himself, though he knew the boys' sudden determination to have adventures and suspected that something of the kind was in the wind now.

"If we flew to California, for instance," said Frank.

"Flew there," repeated Mr. Chester. "My dear boy, how could you do that?"

"In the *Golden Eagle*, of course," exclaimed Harry.

"But—but what for?" questioned the amazed Mr. Chester.

"For a hundred thousand dollars," put in Billy.

"You mean for that newspaper prize?"

The boys nodded.

"I don't like the idea of your entering a contest of that character," said Mr. Chester; "there is a great deal of danger, too."

"No more than we have been through," remonstrated Frank; "besides, think of the experience. Why, we would fly over a dozen states."

"A dozen—fifty, at least," cried Billy, with a fine disregard for geography.

"But how would you go? How long would it take you?" demanded their father.

"I haven't figured out just the time we would consume," said Frank, "but I have a rough idea of our route. The object, of course, would be to avoid any big mountain chains, although if we have our Joyce automatic adjuster I think we could manage even those cross currents with ease. But this is to be a race and we want to get there first. The newspaper route is from here to Pittsburg, from there to Nashville, crossing the Ohio and Cumberland rivers, thence, due west almost, across the northern part of Arkansas, Oklahoma, the Texas Panhandle, New Mexico, Arizona and then across California to San Francisco."

"Hurrah," cried Billy, his eyes shining. "Indians, cowboys, gold mines and oranges."

When the laugh at the jumbled series of images the mention of the different states Frank had enumerated aroused in Billy's mind had died down Mr. Chester wanted to know how the boys were going to carry their supplies.

"Well," said Frank, "as you are going to California and leaving the car behind we thought that perhaps you wouldn't mind letting us use it. We will be very careful — —"

"Oh, very," repeated Harry.

"Most," supplemented Billy.

Mr. Chester laughed.

"I never saw such boys," he said, "but even supposing you had the automobile — I say supposing you had it, could you carry enough supplies in it for the aeroplane?"

"I am sure we could," Frank asserted. "You see, automobiles are in such general use nowadays that it would only be in the desolate parts of the western states that we should have to carry a large supply of gasolene. Almost every village nowadays has it in stock."

"You seem to have the whole thing thought out," laughed Mr. Chester.

"It will be the trip of a lifetime," shouted Harry.

"Well, I shall have to consult with your mother," was Mr. Chester's dictum.

Mrs. Chester objected very much at first to her sons' plan.

"You are always going off on dangerous trips. I do wish you'd spend a little time at home," she said.

But the boys assured her they would be very careful and would keep constantly in touch with their parents by telegraph and not take any unwarranted risks.

"Well, I suppose I shall have to yield," said Mrs. Chester at length.

"Hurrah!" cried the boys.

And thus it came about that one week before the big race across the continent was due to start the names of the Chester Boys were enrolled on the *Planet's* lists as contestants.

CHAPTER VI. OFF FOR SAN FRANCISCO.

The final touches had been put on the *Golden Eagle* and she had been transported to Governor's Island off the Battery four days later. The start for the great transcontinental race was to be made from the flats at the southern end of the reservation. The boys discovered that as the day of the race drew nearer that the list of entrants had narrowed down to three. There was their own aeroplane, the Slade entry of the *Despatch*, and a big dirigible which had also been entered by the *Despatch*. This left them the sole representative of the *Planet*. Of the large number of original entrants, some of them had become discouraged. Others' machines had been broken in practice and still others were convinced, as the starting day drew near, that it would be impracticable to make the long flight.

"Well, the contest is certainly narrowed down," commented Frank one day while they were all seated in front of their shed watching the *Despatch's* plane alight from a flight it had taken above the Jersey meadows.

"I'm glad of it," said Harry; "the fewer there are in the race the easier it will be to avoid collisions and accidents."

After his attempt to steal the plans of Mr. Joyce's gyroscopic balancer the boys heard no more of Fred Reade in a hostile way. Of course, they did not speak, and Reade cast black looks at them as he came and went on his frequent visits to the aerodrome of Arthur Slade. However, his active antagonism seemed to have ceased. Probably he was too busy arranging the final details of the start to be able to spare the time to make himself unpleasant.

The big dirigible, a red painted affair with a crimson gas bag, was also housed on the island. So great was public interest that the little Government steamer that brought visitors over from the mainland was crowded down to her guards with the curious who had obtained passes to see the racing machines.

For her dash overland the *Golden Eagle* had been equipped with her wireless. An outfit of Frank's invention had also been installed in the automobile which was to carry old Mr. Joyce, Lathrop Beasley and Billy

Barnes. Lathrop was an expert operator and the boys hoped to be able to keep in constant touch with each other by means of the apparatus. Mr. Joyce, it had been agreed, was to accompany the expedition as mechanic. His skilled knowledge of aeroplane engines and construction was expected to prove invaluable in case of the breakdowns which the boys knew they must expect on such a voyage.

At last the night came when the red flag with a white ball in the center, which meant the racing ships would start the next day, was run up on the tall flagstaff at the army post. The boys could hardly sleep for excitement and lay awake till late talking over final details. It was agreed that the auto was to "pick up" the aeroplane as it flew over Jersey City. From that time on they would keep in touch by wireless or telegraph all the way across the country, the auto carrying extra supplies, machinery parts and gasolene.

The *Despatch's* aeroplane was also to be followed by an auto in which Fred Reade was to be a passenger, as was also the red-bearded man whose identity was a mystery to the boys. The red dirigible drivers, not being able to afford an auto, had had to depend on luck for gasoline and other supplies en route, although they could carry a good load.

The day of the start dawned fair and still. The bay lay an unruffled sheet of gray water. The flag drooped on its flagstaff. It was ideal flying weather. All the aviators on the island were up early and working over their machines. There were joints to be tightened, stay wires to be carefully inspected, oiling devices to adjust and engines to be turned. This work was impeded a lot by the inquisitive crowds who began to arrive on the first boat.

A detachment of soldiers was finally set to work roping off a space in which, as the time for the start drew near, the air ships were "parked." This relieved the situation and the boys could work unhampered. Billy Barnes, Lathrop and Mr. Joyce started for Jersey early.

"Good luck!" shouted the boys, as they rolled on to the boat in their big auto.

"So long, see you after dinner," cried Billy with a merry wave of the hand.

The boys' parents, relatives and groups of their school friends had come over to see them off, and when the hard and dirty work was finished the boys had their hands full explaining to their young friends all about the *Golden Eagle*.

At last the bugle that announced that it was half an hour before starting time sounded. An electric wave of enthusiasm ran through the crowd. Over in the city windows of skyscrapers began to fill with men and women anxious to watch the contestants shoot into the air. On ferry boats and roofs all along the water front thousands of eyes were watching.

"Are you all ready?"

It was General Stanton, commander of the Department of the East, who had consented to start the race, who spoke.

"Yes," came in a shout from the aviators.

The dirigible men began to cast off ropes and the aeroplanes were dropped into position. A squad of men drove back the pressing crowds, and the boys, after kissing their parents and bidding farewell to their relatives and friends, took their seats in the *Golden Eagle's* chassis.

There was a mighty roar and blue flames and smoke spouted from the engine exhausts as the motors were started. Men, with their heels dug into the sandy ground to avoid slipping, held back the struggling planes. The dirigible swayed and tugged at her resting ropes like an impatient horse.

"Bang!"

It was the starting gun at last.

"Hurrah!" roared the crowd.

"They're off!" shouted everybody, as if there could be any doubt of it.

"They're off!" shouted everybody.

Like mighty birds the two aeroplanes swept swiftly forward a few yards over the level ground and then headed out far above the river toward the Jersey shore. The big dirigible, its engine droning like an enormous scarab beetle, followed, keeping well up with the speedy winged craft.

From thousands of windows, banked with white faces, handkerchiefs and flags waved and from the roofs of the office buildings housing the *Planet* and *Despatch* plants bombs were exploded at regular intervals to spread the news broadcast that the race had begun. In the offices of the evening papers the great presses were already rushing out "Extras" telling of the start. Soon newsboys in the canyon-like streets of lower New York would be crying their wares.

Every pilot of every boat on the river pulled his whistle cord and tied it down as the air craft swept far above. The uproar was literally ear-splitting. Owing to the roar of their engines, however, the aviators heard little of the turmoil which they caused.

In a few minutes Jersey City, which had gone just as airship mad as New York, was reached. On swept the high-flying craft above its crowded roofs and bellowing factory whistles. Far beneath them they could see the flat green expanse of the meadows beyond with the silver paths marked on them by the Hackensack and Passaic rivers. As they flew onward and left the city far behind the boys could spy on the road beneath them the two convoying autos.

All at once the wireless began to crackle.

"They are sending up a message," exclaimed Harry.

"Great start—good work—we'll beat them all to a frazzle," was the message the spark spelled out.

"Thank you, let's hope so," replied Harry.

The course had been marked on maps that both the Boy Aviators and their companions had handy for reference. From the autos, too, flew red and blue flags, which made identification easy. At night the Boy Aviators' auto was to burn red lights. The signal that a good landing place was at hand would be flashed upward at night by a blue flare. Of course, if it was necessary to alight in the daytime the occupants of the *Golden Eagle* would be able to spy such spots far below them more readily than anyone driving on the surface.

The engine was working perfectly as the *Golden Eagle* rushed onward. Its steady song delighted the young voyagers. Harry, with watchful eyes, looked after the lubrication, while Frank kept the craft steady on her course. On and on they flew, the autos beneath seeming specks in clouds of dust. The dirigible was about two miles behind and the *Despatch's* aeroplane was a short distance in front of it. The boys, therefore, had a good lead.

"That's a good start. We're beating them already," exclaimed Harry.

Frank smiled.

"Two miles isn't much in a race of this length," he remarked. "We've only started, Harry. We'll have lots of ups and downs before we've finished."

How prophetic his words were neither of the boys realized at that time.

CHAPTER VII. ABOVE THE EARTH.

As it grew dusk the boys found themselves flying high above a pleasant wooded country, dotted here and there with small villages and prosperous looking farms. From their lofty station they could see men and women rush out below them waving their arms in excited amazement as the contestants in the big race swept along. Cattle and horses, too, tore about their pastures mad with terror at what they doubtless thought were terrible destroying birds of enormous size.

Occasionally, too, they would fly above rivers and railroads and by noting these carefully they managed to keep their bearings clear. The *Despatch* aeroplane was now far behind and the dirigible had taken up second place. The auto had been lost sight of also.

"Send out a wireless. We must locate Billy and the others," said Frank.

The instrument clicked off the message, its blue spark leaping and crackling across the gap like a tongue of living fire.

In a few minutes a reply came back.

"We are now passing Cresston, Pennsylvania. Land and wait for us at Remson. You can tell it by its red brick church tower."

"There it is off there to the north about five miles," cried Harry, pointing to where a tall red tower stood out against the sky.

"I hope we can find a good landing place there," said Frank, setting his rudder over a bit. The airship answered like an obedient steed. Round to the north she swung, her gyroscopic balancing device keeping her from heeling over, even at the sharp angle at which Frank guided her round.

As they drew near Remson the greatest excitement prevailed. People could be seen scurrying out in all directions and pointing upward. Suddenly a deep-toned "ding-dong" was borne upward to the young sky navigators.

"They are ringing the church bell to announce our arrival," cried Frank.

"Well, I hope they've got supper ready for us," laughed Harry; "air-riding gives me an appetite like a horse."

A few hundred yards from the center of the town was a flat green field which made an ideal landing place. Frank swept downward toward it and as the townsfolk saw that the aeroplane was going to drop there was a mighty rush of townsfolk. The road leading to the field was black with them. The younger ones climbed fences and cut across lots to get there in time.

Frank saw that unless they got out of the way there was going to be trouble. He shouted to them to clear a path, but either from stupidity or from ignorance of aeroplanes they stood stolidly gazing upward, open mouthed, as the aeroplane rushed down.

"Out of the way!" yelled Frank.

"Hurray!" cried the people, not budging an inch.

There was only one thing to do to avoid injuring someone and that was to attempt to land at the further end of the field where there were some trees. This meant a risk of smashing the *Golden Eagle* or at least damaging her, but if loss of life was to be avoided it was the only course to pursue.

With a ripping, rending sound, as the twigs and branches grazed her, the big plane dropped to earth.

There was a sharp, snapping sound, as her landing wheels struck the ground. A branch had caught one of the rudder-guide wires and torn it out, breaking a pulley wire. Worse still, one of the wheels was badly damaged. But the crowd minded none of this. They rushed in and began handling the aeroplane, pulling wires and twisting wheels and levers, till the boys began to despair of ever getting their craft away from Remson intact.

All at once, however, a big red-faced man appeared and began angrily driving the people back. He was the owner of the field, it seemed, and was dressed like a farmer. When by dint of threatening them with the constable he had succeeded in getting the crowd to fall back to a respectful distance, he began to ply the boys with questions.

They were too busy examining the damage done to their craft to answer many of them, and the man doubtless thought them a very surly pair of youths.

In a few minutes the auto drove up and there was more excitement.

"What's happened?" asked Billy, as soon as the three occupants of the car reached the boys' side.

"A bit of bad luck," said Frank, straightening up from his scrutiny of the damage.

"Let me look at it, boys," said old Mr. Joyce, who had spent the whole trip over his beloved calculations.

He crawled in under the plane, and soon emerged again, shaking his head.

"We'll have to get a new wheel," he said. "If I had wire, a tire and tools, I could invent one, but I haven't."

"But where can we get one?" gasped Harry, for spare wheels were one of the necessities the boys had forgotten to put in the auto.

"A bicycle wheel would do," said Mr. Joyce, who was seated on the grass designing an improved mousetrap.

Inquiry developed the fact that nobody in Remson was willing to sell a bicycle wheel, and the boys were almost in despair until one of the villagers volunteered the information that there was a bicycle factory at Tottenville, twenty miles away.

"We'll have to go over there in the auto. That's the only thing to do," announced Frank.

"Looks like it," agreed the others.

An arrangement was made with the red-faced man whereby the boys leased a bit of his field for a camping-place for the night, and the waterproof tent was soon erected, the portable cots set up, and the blue-flame stove started going under a liberal supply of ham and eggs and coffee. Lathrop went into the village and soon returned with pie and cakes. The boys' meal was rather a public one, for the villagers seemed hypnotized by the sight of the sky boys, and gazed stolidly at them as they ate, as if there was something as wonderful in that as in their flights.

While they were eating, a farmer, who had driven into town from a small village some miles away, announced that the dirigible and the *Despatch* aeroplane had landed there.

"Well, we are holding our lead, anyway," remarked Harry cheerfully.

"I hope we can maintain it as far as Pittsburg," said Frank, for, of course, all the contestants had to race over the prescribed course.

As soon as supper had been despatched the boys got into the auto, leaving old Mr. Joyce to guard the aeroplane, and, after making inquiries about the road, started off for Tottenville. The road was a straight one, and there was a bright, full moon, so they did not anticipate any difficulty in arriving at their destination. Before they started Frank 'phoned to the factory, and an assortment of wheels was left for them in charge of the watchman, as the factory would be closed for the night long before they could reach there.

Frank sent the auto bounding over the road at a fast clip. Their lights shone brightly in front of them, showing them the track for some distance ahead.

"Look there!" suddenly shouted Lathrop, as they swept down a steep hill.

Directly in the road in front of them the headlights revealed a big, lumbering hay-wagon, loaded high with its sweet-smelling burden.

"Hey, get out of the road!" shouted Frank at the top of his voice.

But the man on the wagon seemed to be asleep. Anyway he paid no attention to the boys' loud hail, but kept serenely on in the middle of the road. His big lumbering wagon quite prohibited all chance of passing him.

"Stop the machine," cried Harry.

Frank shoved on the emergency brake. But instead of the auto coming to a stop there was a sharp snap as if something had broken.

"It's busted," cried Frank. "I can't stop the car."

"Now we are in for it," exclaimed Harry.

On rushed the auto, gathering speed as it tore down the hill.

Suddenly the man on the hay-wagon awoke, and, looking back to ascertain the cause of all the noise behind him, saw the car bearing down on him.

"Stop it!" he shouted.

"I can't!" yelled back Frank.

"Oh, we'll all be killed," cried Lathrop.

But the man was shouting something and pointing ahead.

"What's he saying?" asked Billy through his chattering teeth.

"He says if we don't stop we'll all be killed. There's a bridge ahead and only room for one vehicle on it."

As Frank spoke, the boys saw the bridge, a narrow, wooden affair. The road widened a particle just before it reached the bridge. The arch spanned a quite wide creek, the water in which sparkled brightly in the moonlight. Dumb with alarm the boys sat helplessly in the onrushing auto. Frank gripped the wheel and desperately cast about for some way to get out of the difficulty.

Suddenly he almost gave a shout. To one side of the bridge he saw that the banks of the stream were low and sloped gently. It might be possible to run the auto across the stream that way.

At any rate he decided to try.

As the auto reached the point at which the road widened, the boy swung the speeding machine over and whizzed by the wagon so closely that wisps of hay clung to the auto's side.

But the lead horses—there were four of them—blocked access to the bridge.

The next minute there was a shout of alarm from the boys, as they saw that Frank meant to dash across the stream. The auto struck the bank, seemed to bound into the air, and then crashed down into the water with a force that threw a cloud of spray high above it and thoroughly drenched its occupants.

But to Frank's great joy the machine did not overturn, nor did it seem damaged, as it kept right on through the water, which, luckily, was not deep, and dashed up the other bank. Here Frank managed to get it under control—as the opposite side of the creek was a steep grade—and the car came to a stop with a grunt and a groan.

"Gee whilikens, I thought you was all killed for sure," exclaimed the badly frightened countryman, as he drove up to the group of boys, who were out of their car by this time and busily examining the extent of the accident to the emergency brake.

"It wasn't your fault we weren't," blurted out the indignant Billy. "You are a fine driver to go to sleep like that."

"Don't you sass me, young feller," roared the countryman; "what business have you got to be flying around the roads in that choo-choo cart and scaring folks out of their wits?"

"Just as much as you have to be occupying the whole road and going to sleep like that," retorted Billy.

"I've a good mind to give you a licking, young feller," said the man, starting to climb down from his wagon. But he thought better of it, as he saw the four determined looking boys standing there in the moonlight.

"I'll fix you later," he muttered. "Git up, Sal; git up, Ned," and he cracked his whip and the wagon rumbled on up the hill.

A short survey showed the boys that the damage done to the brake could be repaired with a few turns with the monkey-wrench, one of the bolts having worked loose. The adjustment made, they climbed back into the car, and were soon speeding once more toward Tottenville.

At the factory they found the watchman waiting for them, with several new wheels of the stoutest make.

"You're in luck," he said, as the boys paid for the one they selected and gave him something for his trouble besides. "This wheel was made for one of them air-ship bugs that lived in this town. He bruk his neck before it could be delivered, and it's lain here ever since."

The boys agreed that however unfortunate it had been for the luckless Tottenville aviator, it was good luck for them, and after thanking the man they started back for Remson at a fast clip.

As they bowled along they passed a ruinous looking hut, in which, late as was the hour, a light was burning.

"That's funny," said Frank.

"What's funny?" inquired Billy.

"Why, to see a light burning in a tumble-down hut like that at such an hour. Folk in the country go to bed early as a rule; and see there, there's an automobile in front of the house."

Sure enough, a big touring car, with its lights burning brightly, was drawn up in front of the hut, which lay back at some distance from the road.

"It is queer," agreed Harry.

As the boy spoke they all started at an unexpected happening.

From the hut there came a piercing cry of:

"Help!"

CHAPTER VIII. BOY AVIATORS TO THE RESCUE.

"They are murdering some one in there!" cried Frank, bringing the car to a stop.

Indeed, the piercing cries indicated that some one was being maltreated, if not actually murdered.

"Come on, we'll save him," cried Harry, drawing his revolver, for all the boys had thought it best to carry arms on such a trip as they were undertaking.

"Be careful. We had better peek through that window first, and see with whom we have to deal before we announce our presence," breathed Frank, as the boys tiptoed up the path.

"That's a good idea," agreed Billy. "There might be a lot of them and then we should have to get help."

Cautiously they crept up the path and peered in at the window of the deserted hut. A strange scene met their eyes.

In one corner of the bare room a rugged man with a grizzled beard was tied hand and foot, while another man with a red-hot poker seemed about to burn his eyes out. His cries for help were pitiful.

His captors, however—for beside the man with the poker there were two other men in the room—seemed to have no pity for him. The man with the poker was exclaiming in a fierce voice:

"Sign the title to the mine or we will kill you," as the boys peeked cautiously into the room, which was lighted by a lamp detached from the auto. On the tumble-down hearth the fire in which the poker had been heated smouldered.

The man with the poker had his back to the boys, but even about that there seemed something strangely familiar. The appealing words next uttered by the bound man soon apprised them with whom they had to deal.

"I will never do so, Luther Barr," declared the victim in a trembling voice.

The boys all started with amazement at encountering their old enemy in such a surprising manner in this out-of-the-way hut at midnight.

"Your attempts to get the papers from me are of no use. Kill me if you must, but don't torture me."

"So you won't tell where they are," cried Barr angrily.

"I will not," said his victim firmly.

"Then take that," cried Barr, in a cruel tone.

The horrified boys saw him lunge forward with the red-hot iron. His victim gave a loud cry of pain as he felt the red-hot metal approach his eyes to burn them out; but even as Barr raised his arm Frank had decided what to do.

"Stop that!" he cried in a loud, clear voice.

As Frank had expected, this sudden interruption so startled the miscreants that they at once left their victim and started for the door. As they rushed toward the portal, Frank, with a cry of "Come on," leaped through the window frame, from which the glass sash had long ago been broken, and followed by the others, was in the room the next instant.

"Quick, Harry; cut him loose," he ordered, handing the other boy a big hunting knife.

It was only the work of a few seconds to free the man. But before the ropes had fallen from him Luther Barr and the two other men had rushed back from the door and made a dash at the boys.

"Stay where you are, Mr. Barr," said Frank, leveling his revolver; "I don't want to hurt you."

"What, you interfering whelps, have you crossed my path again?" shouted Barr, who had recognized the boys instantly. "This time I'll fix you for interfering with my plans."

He suddenly whipped out a revolver and fired point-blank at Frank. The bullet whistled past the boy's ears and buried itself behind him.

The next instant the room was plunged into sudden darkness. One of Luther Barr's companions, in stepping backward to get a rifle that leaned against the wall, had knocked the light over.

"Quick, boys, run for the auto," shouted Frank, taking advantage of this sudden diversion.

Before the others could recover their wits, the boys, half dragging the man they had rescued with them, reached the door, and the next minute were in their auto.

"Shoot at their tires," they heard old Barr shout, as they whizzed off down the road.

A shower of bullets followed, some of which struck the tonneau. But none of the missiles, fortunately, either wounded them or hit the tires, in which latter case they would have had to come to a standstill.

Frank put on full speed, and with the start they already had they soon outdistanced the auto which held Barr and his two companions. It followed them for a short distance, however, old Barr shouting maledictions after them.

"Oh, how can I ever thank you boys?" exclaimed the rescued man, as he gratefully clasped Frank's arm. "That terrible man, Luther Barr, would certainly have blinded, and perhaps killed me, if you had not arrived in time."

"How did you come to get in his power?" asked Frank.

"It is a long story, young man, and begins in Arizona," said the stranger; "but first, I must tell you my name is Bart Witherbee, and I am well known in the West as a prospector. I located a valuable mine, which seems abandoned, some time ago in the northern part of the state, and I have managed to keep the location a secret till I can file a formal claim to it. In some way the two men whom you saw with Barr to-night, and who are Hank Higgins and Noggy Wilkes, two bad men, and gamblers, heard of this. They formerly worked for Barr, who has mining property in Arizona. When they learned I was coming to New York to see my daughter, they came along, too, and informed Barr of what they knew about the valuable mine I had found. At that time I did not know Barr, and by these two men was tricked into meeting him on the pretense that he had some real estate he was willing to trade for mines in Arizona. I have other claims beside the one I located recently, and I thought I might trade one of them for some of Barr's property in the East.

"You can imagine my consternation when we arrived out here to find myself in the hands of Hank Higgins and Noggy Wilkes. I tried to run, but they caught and tied me, and, as you saw, would have either killed me or maimed me for life if you hadn't saved me."

"What part of Arizona is your mine in?" asked Harry, deeply interested, as they all were, in the man's narrative.

"It is near to a place called Calabazos, in the northern part of the state near the Black Cañon," replied the man. "I want to let you boys have a share of it for what you have done for me to-night. It would be only a slight return."

"Why, we are going near to Calabazos," exclaimed Billy. "I noticed it on the map. It's near the Black Cañon."

"That's right, young feller," said the miner; "but what are you tenderfoots going to do out there?"

Frank explained about the transcontinental flight.

"Wow," cried the westerner, "that's going some, for fair. Well, boys, I'm going to get on the fastest train I can and get back to Calabazos, and file my claim, for you can call me a Chinese chop-stick if that thar Luther Barr isn't going to camp on my trail till he finds where the mine is located."

"I guess you are right," remarked Frank. "Luther Barr won't stop at anything when he starts out to accomplish a purpose."

"Why, you talk as if you knew him," exclaimed the astonished miner.

"Know him?" echoed Billy with a laugh. "I should say we do, eh, boys?"

The boys' previous acquaintance with the unscrupulous old man was soon explained to Bart Witherbee, who interrupted the narrative at frequent intervals with whistles of astonishment and loud exclamations of, "Wall, I swan"; "Call me a jack-rabbit, now," "If that don't beat hunting coyotes with a sling-shot," and other exclamations that seemed peculiar to himself.

"Wall, now, boys, you've got to have some part of that mine, if only for the sake of getting even with that old man."

The boys tried to insist that they had no right to any of Witherbee's property, but he was so insistent that finally they consented to visit the mine with him when they reached Calabazos, that is, if they were far enough ahead in the race to be able to spare a few hours.

Witherbee told them some of his history. He was the son of a stage-coach driver, who had been killed by robbers. The miner, after the murder, had been adopted by somebody whose name he could not recollect. It seemed that some years after his adoption he had been kidnapped by a traveling circus, and had sustained a severe blow on the head by falling from a high trapeze. This made him forget everything but his very early youth. After a while he escaped from the circus and joined a camp of miners. He had been a miner ever since.

"I've often thought I'd like to meet the man who cared for me when my father was killed," he said, "fer he was good ter me, I remember. Sometimes I have a flash of memory and can almost recollect his name, but it always slips me at last. If he ever met me, though, he'd know me all right. See this?" He rolled up his sleeve and showed them a livid scar. "I was on the coach when it was attacked, and that's a souvenir I got. They didn't mean to hit me, it was just a stray bullet."

"And your mother," asked Frank, "is not she alive?"

"She was killed, too, the night the robbers attacked the stage," said the miner softly. "She was sitting by my father when the attack came."

They reached their camp without further incident, and found that Mr. Joyce had sat up for them and had a hot supper ready. That they did justice to the meal after their exciting adventures of the night, you may be sure. The meal disposed of, the adventurers turned in for a few hours of badly needed sleep.

"Our adventures seem to have begun with a vengeance," sleepily remarked Billy Barnes, as he was dozing off.

"Do you think we shall see any more of Luther Barr?" asked Harry.

"It wouldn't surprise me," rejoined Frank. "He is not the kind of man not to seek vengeance for the rebuff we gave him to-night."

51

CHAPTER IX. LUTHER BARR FORMS AN ALLIANCE.

At daybreak Frank was out of his cot and after dashing cold water over himself — the liquid being carried from a clear stream in a neighboring field in a bucket he aroused his companions and breakfast was soon sending an appetizing odor into the air. The boys fell to with hearty appetites, and after leaving several telegrams and post cards to be forwarded to their friends and parents in New York, they started actively in on preparations for the resumption of their long journey. The new wheel was soon fitted, and found to answer perfectly. The broken wire was also soon adjusted.

The work had just been completed and the auto and aeroplane fed with fresh gasolene, lubricants and water when Witherbee, the miner, who had slept at a hotel in the village, came hurrying up.

"Call me a horn-toad of the sagebrush desert if here ain't a go, boys!" he exclaimed.

The boys looked up at their new friend and saw that his face was pale and he looked dismayed.

"Whatever is the matter?" they demanded.

"Matter?" echoed the miner; "call me a gila monster if that there dodgasted Barr and his companions ain't stolen my pocketbook."

"Did it have much money in it?" asked Frank in a sympathetic tone, for the poor miner's distress was very real.

"Why, it had two hundred dollars. All I have till I can get back to Arizonee. Call me a doodelbug, if that ain't tough luck."

"It certainly is," sympathized Harry; "perhaps we could lend you — —"

"Not a cent," broke in the miner. "Bart Witherbee ain't borrowing money from kids. But if you'd give me a seat in that benzine buggy of yours I'll be grateful to you for the rest of my life. Maybe I can help you, too, in the far west. You see, I know that country, and if we run into any bad Indians or cowboys, I can maybe be of some use to you."

"That's so," agreed Frank; "do you think there would be room in the auto, Billy?"

"Sure," replied the young reporter. "If there isn't, we'll make it. We can't leave Bart Witherbee here penniless."

"Say, boys, it was the luckiest day of my life when I struck you — call me a comical coyote, if it warn't!" exclaimed the miner gratefully. "But I'll make it all up to you when I locate my mine."

The red-faced man from whom they had leased their camping-place readily agreed to take charge of their letters and telegrams. Indeed, any one in the crowd that gathered to see the start of the boy aviators on the second day of their long trip would have been willing to do anything for them in their enthusiasm over the daring young adventurers.

With a cheer from the crowd the auto bowled off first, vanishing down the road to the west in a cloud of dust. Hardly had it started when there was a loud whirring noise, and down the road came two other motor cars. In the first sat Fred Reade and the red-bearded man, who acted as his assistant, it seemed. In the other, to the boys' amazement, rode Luther Barr and his two companions of the night before — the western gamblers. Apparently Barr and Reade were on friendly terms, for, as the two machines shot by, Reade turned back in the tonneau and shouted something to Barr, who answered with a wave of the hand.

"Hullo! That looks bad," exclaimed Harry, as the cars shot by.

"What does?" asked Frank, who had been busy adjusting the engine, and had not seen the motor cars.

"Why, Reade and Barr seem to have joined forces. Depend upon it they are up to some mischief."

Had the boys known that the night before Luther Barr and the two others had been guests at Reade's camp, they would have had even more reason to feel apprehensive. In his chase after the Boy Aviators and Bart Witherbee, old Barr had mistaken the road and branched off down a sidetrack that soon brought him to Reade's camp, where he and his companions were working over their aeroplane by kerosene flares. The old millionaire recognized Reade at once, stopped and hailed him.

Reade soon explained to him that he was in the aeroplane race as the representative of the *Despatch*. On Barr inquiring how he came to leave the *Planet*, Reade explained that his leaving was due to Billy Barnes.

"That interfering cub lost me my job," he said angrily.

Old Barr was interested at once. Here was another enemy of the Boy Aviators. Perhaps it would be possible to join forces to harass them.

"I see you like the boys as little as I do," he ventured cautiously.

"Like them," exclaimed Reade angrily, "I hate them. I hope they lose this race. I mean to prevent them winning by fair means or foul, if I can."

"Good," was Barr's reply; "that's just the way I feel about it. Now I have a proposition to make to you."

There followed a long conversation in low tones, the result of which was that old Barr agreed to accompany the *Despatch's* party as far as Arizona and the mine, the location of which Witherbee was hiding. He had instantly made up his mind that Reade was a valuable ally.

"I am sure that Witherbee means to let those boys know where the mine is, and give them part of it," he declared; "and if we can find it first, we can divide it among ourselves."

Luther Barr had no intention of giving away any part of the mine if he found it. He wanted it all for himself. But he thought that to hold out such a tempting bait would make Reade an even more faithful ally. As for the reporter, he was delighted to have found an enemy of the Boy Aviators. He was a coward, and had been afraid that his party was too small to openly cause them much trouble. Now, however, he was highly pleased at the idea of traveling in such powerful company, and promised himself a "lot of fun with those young cubs."

And so it came about that Luther Barr and the *Despatch* auto traveled in company when they broke camp the next morning.

The two autos had hardly passed down the road and out of sight when a shout from the crowd announced that the aeroplane of Arthur Slade was in sight.

"Come on, we've got no time to lose," cried Frank, as he saw the rival aeroplane coming rapidly into view.

Both boys scrambled into their craft, and a moment later, amid a roar from the crowd, they shot upward. As they did so, Slade shot by. He was a powerfully built man, with a mean expression of countenance, and seemed to harbor a spite against the boys, doubtless because he did not like to be pitted against such youthful antagonists.

"I'll win this race hands down," he shouted, as he swept by.

As the boys' aeroplane gathered velocity, however, they overhauled him, and all day the two air-craft fought it out desperately. There seemed to be little difference between them, and the boys resolved that they were in for the tussle of their lives if they meant to win the race. The dirigible hung doggedly on, about three miles in the rear. Her crew did not seem to be urging her. Doubtless they reasoned that in a race of such length it was a good plan to husband their resources and not urge their ship forward too fast.

"The gasolene is running low," announced Harry, shortly after noon, "and we need some more oil."

"All right; send out a wireless, and we'll drop in a convenient place," replied Frank.

The auto was some distance behind, but a reply to Harry's message soon flashed back to the occupants of the aeroplane, and a few minutes after they had landed in a smooth, green meadow the auto came chugging up. The tank was replenished, and a hasty luncheon eaten. By this time both the rival aeroplane and the dirigible were out of sight. As the boys had seen nothing further of the autos occupied by Reade and Luther Barr, they concluded they must be traveling on another road — which was, in fact, the case.

"Aren't you scared to let the other aeroplane get such a long lead?" asked Billy, as the boys made ready to resume their flight.

"They won't get very far," said Frank lightly. "You see, they will have to come down for fresh gasolene, just as we did. They have got an air-cooled engine, too, and if they run it too long it will get heated and stop, so that they will have to quit for a while, too."

"How about the dirigible?"

"The only chance it has to win this race is for both the aeroplanes to break down," said Harry. "We can pass it even if it got a twenty-mile lead."

The *Golden Eagle* flew on during the afternoon without incident. It was getting toward sundown, and Frank was thinking of descending and camping for the night, when, as they were passing high above a spot where four cross-roads intersected, they spied below them the two autos of Barr and Reade drawn up near to the rival aeroplane, which, as Frank had said, had been compelled to come down to replenish her tanks.

Through his glasses Harry scrutinized the group. They were gathered about Slade's aeroplane, and seemed to be discussing excitedly.

"I thought so," said Harry, as he put the glasses back in their pocket at the side of the pilot house.

"Thought what?" asked Frank.

"Why, I guess there's something the matter with their cylinders. Overheated, I guess. They were pouring water on them when I looked through the glass."

Hardly had he spoken when there was a singing sound in the air close by his ear. It was like the droning of a big June bug.

"Pretty high for a bug to be flying," commented Harry.

"That wasn't any bug, Harry," contradicted Frank, "it was a bullet."

"What! they are firing at us again?"

"Evidently."

There came another whistling in the air, as a second projectile whizzed by.

"We ought to have them arrested," exclaimed Harry indignantly.

"How are we to prove who fired the shots?" rejoined Frank.

He was right. At the time they whizzed by the aeroplane was over a clump of woods which effectually concealed from her occupants the identity of the wielder of the rifle. Barr's party had evidently speeded their autos in under the trees and were firing from them. No more bullets came, however. Probably the shooters saw the futility of trying to get good aim through the thick foliage.

Camp that night was made beside a small river, in which Witherbee soon caught a fine mess of yellow perch. These, cooked with the old plainsman's skill, made an agreeable variation from the usual camp fare, and were despatched by the hungry boys in an incredibly short time.

Of the other aeroplane they had seen nothing since they passed her in the afternoon.

"This means we get a good long lead," rejoiced Frank.

But the boys were doomed to disappointment, for shortly before midnight the whirring noise of an engine was heard overhead, and, looking upward, the adventurers, awakened by Billy, who was on watch, saw a dark body pass overhead.

"It's Slade's machine!" cried Frank.

Shortly afterward the dirigible also went by, with several lights displayed about her decks. The boys shot up a ray of light from the searchlight on the auto, and were greeted by a cheer from the men on the dirigible.

"Well, if those fellows think they can steal a night march on us, we'll fool 'em," exclaimed Frank. "Here, Harry, let's have a look at that map. I must lay out a course, and then we'll get after them. You fellows break camp and be ready to follow us in the auto."

There was a lot of bustle and excitement while Frank, by the light of an auto-lamp, with compasses, dividers and measured rule, worked out a course. A route was soon devised.

"All ready?" he cried at last, when final directions had been given.

"All ready," said Billy, tightening the ropes that held the tarpaulin covering the supplies in the auto.

"Then we're off," cried Frank, as he and Harry jumped into the *Golden Eagle*, and with a rattling roar of explosions glided into the air.

CHAPTER X. A NIGHT VOYAGE.

Sailing through the air at night is a vastly different thing to the delightful exhilaration of a day voyage. In the latter case, all is plain going—provided, of course, the weather conditions are right—below the aviator is spread out, like a many-colored carpet, a glowing landscape dotted with peaceful hamlets, busy smoky cities, and quiet farms and patches of woodland. But at night all is changed. The darkness hangs about the driving air-craft like a pall. The aviator anxiously scans the earth below him for an occasional light or the glare that a distant city casts on the sky. It is by those means alone that he can get his bearings, unless he is a skilled navigator and steers by the compass. Even then he may get lost. All is uncertainty.

So intent on overtaking their rivals, however, were the boys, that they reckoned little of the risks they ran, and kept the *Golden Eagle* headed on an almost due westerly course. The tiny shaded light above the binnacle was the only speck of illumination about the air-ship. Luckily the moon cast a bright, white illumination, but the luminary was waning, and was already low in the western sky. Soon all would be as black as a well.

"Heard anything from the auto?" asked Frank, with a backward glance, after they had been running about an hour thus.

"Not a thing," rejoined Harry; "that means they must have a light in sight."

"Still, I should like to know just where they are. Send them a flash."

Harry bent over the wireless key and sent a message crackling into the night:

"Send up a flare."

The answer soon came. From far below them a blue illumination lit up the trees and along a stretch of road in a lurid glare. The amused young aviators could see horses and cattle out at pasture in the quiet fields galloping for dear life at the alarming apparition.

"Can you see any sign of the others?" asked Frank, some minutes later.

Both boys had in the interval been peering anxiously ahead into the night.

"Not a sign, can you?"

"Not yet."

"We ought to catch sight of them soon."

"That's so. We should have no difficulty in making out the dirigible, illuminated as she is."

The boys lapsed into silence, straining their eyes ahead in vain.

Suddenly Harry gave a shout.

"There she is, about four points off our course to the north."

"That's right. That's the dirigible, sure enough. Now, comparing her speed with that of Slade's machine, he cannot be far off."

"Say, we've been making time, all right."

"I should say we have. But look! Something's the matter with the dirigible."

As Harry spoke they saw the row of lights by which they had picked the gas-supported craft out of the night suddenly waver and then begin to drop.

"They are going to descend," cried Harry amazedly.

"Evidently. Look there!" he broke off with a sharp exclamation.

A red glare suddenly enveloped the dirigible, showing her every outline.

"It's a distress signal!" was the elder lad's excited shout. "Something has happened."

"I'll tell the boys in the auto to answer it," suggested Harry.

He sent out a sputtering wireless, which was soon answered by a blue glare from the auto. An answering illumination from the dirigible went up.

"They've seen our signal," cried Frank. "Now, Harry, switch on the searchlight."

"What for?"

"To pick out a landing-place by. I don't want to risk our necks by dropping in the dark."

"You are going to land and help them?"

"Of course; they may be in serious trouble. It is our duty to aid them."

"But Slade's machine?"

"Well, he'll make a big gain on us to-night, I'm afraid, but it can't be helped. They have signaled for assistance, and we've got to go to their help."

The white finger of light of the searchlight began to sweep the ground below them. So far as they could see, they were traveling over a cleared country only interspersed here and there by clumps of trees.

"This looks as good a place to drop as any," said Frank as he scrutinized the nature of the country over which they were soaring in slow circles.

Harry assented.

"Tell me when to cut out the engine," he said.

"I'll do that myself," replied Frank. "I'll do it with the emergency cut-outs. We might have to shift up again in a hurry, and the engine acts more quickly on the driving wheel controls."

The aeroplane began to drop. About a quarter of a mile from her the dirigible was settling, too. Her crew kept burning flares so as to see that they didn't blunder into any growth that might have ripped their gas bag.

The boys reached the earth without a mishap, and found themselves in a rocky meadow, about a hundred yards from the road. In a few minutes the auto came chugging along with an excited party on board.

"What is it?"

"What has happened?"

"What's the matter?"

"Call me a tenderfoot if I didn't think it was Pain's fireworks."

The exclamations and questions came in a perfect volley.

"One at a time, one at a time," laughed Frank; "we're not phonographs."

"You scared the life out of us," interjected Billy Barnes.

"Well, you needn't worry about the *Golden Eagle*; with the exception of the time we are losing, she is as sound as a bell, but the dirigible over yonder is in some distress. We had better hop in the auto and drive in that direction."

Luckily the road went in the direction in which the dirigible had last been seen, and a short distance down the main track the boys found a field path leading off into an enclosure in which they could see men scurrying round the big dirigible with lanterns in their hands. They seemed much perturbed, and the boys could hear their loud expressions of disgust at their sudden stoppage.

"Dirigible ahoy!" hailed Frank, as the auto rolled up; "what's the trouble?"

"Oh, hello — are you the Boy Aviators?" said a pleasant-faced man, whom the boys recognized as James McArthur, the driver and owner of the craft. "It's mighty good of you to come to our aid. Yes, we've cracked a propeller blade, and are in a bad fix. You see, we lost a lot of gas in dropping, and that means we'll have to lighten the ship."

"I hope it doesn't put you out of the race," sympathized Frank; "it's too bad such an accident should have occurred."

"It is, indeed," said Mr. McArthur. "We were doing so well, too."

"If you will let us I think we can help you out," volunteered Frank.

"If you only could," exclaimed the other eagerly.

"We've got a spare propeller in the auto. If you like, I can let you have it till you reach Pittsburg or some town where you can get a new one fitted."

"Oh, I couldn't think of depriving you."

"Not at all. I don't think there is a chance of our having any accident to our propellers. You are welcome to it."

Mr. McArthur, with profuse expressions of thanks, thereupon gratefully accepted the propeller which the boys unpacked from its place in the big tonneau of their car. It was not long before it was bolted in place, and the dirigible ready to start. The new propeller was a trifle smaller than the old one, but the driver of the dirigible was confident he could get good results with it. Before he started, however, he had to drop three of his men, with instructions to them to walk to the nearest town and then take the train for Pittsburg, at which city he could get fresh supplies of hydrogen gas. In the meantime McArthur and one man were to handle the dirigible, and almost every bit of ballast she carried was sacrificed.

Amid a perfect tornado of thanks, which they would have been glad to dodge, the boys hurried back to the *Golden Eagle*, and were soon once more in the air. Daybreak found them flying about nine hundred feet above a hilly, sparsely settled country.

As the light grew brighter, which it did slowly, with a promise of rain, they gazed eagerly about them in every direction. Far behind them they could see the tiny speck of the dirigible, laboring along with her small propeller, but of the Slade machine there was not a sign.

"Well, he has got a start of us this time, for fair," exclaimed Harry, as the boys looked blankly at each other, following the result of their scrutiny.

"There's nothing to do but keep doggedly on," rejoined Frank, "but we ought to reach Pittsburg to-night. It looks as if we are in for a rain-storm, too."

"It certainly does," rejoined Harry. "Well, there's one consolation, Slade can't do any better in the rain than we can."

"No, that's so," rejoined Frank, but there was little elation in his tone.

For a time the boys sat in silence. It was broken by a sharp shout from Harry.

"Frank! Frank! look there!"

They were flying above a farm-house, from the chimney of which a cheerful column of smoke was ascending. Hungry and tired as the boys were, they could in imagination smell the breakfast coffee, the aroma of the frizzling bacon and the hiss of the frying eggs. But what had caused Harry's shout was clear enough. Outside the farm-house stood two automobiles, which they recognized as those of Barr and Fred Reade, and a short distance from the two cars stood the *Despatch's* aeroplane.

"They've stopped for breakfast," exultingly cried Frank; "here's where we get ahead of them."

CHAPTER XI. THE FIRST LEG.

The country now began to be more thickly settled. In fact, the boys passed a constant series of surprised villages and frightened farms. While they were passing above one hillside farm, in fact, they were received with a demonstration of more than surprise. A man in blue jeans came running out into his barnyard with a shot-gun, and fired the contents of both barrels upward at the young navigators. At the height they were flying, however, a shot-gun could not harm them.

A short time later Harry lay down for a nap, after both boys had eaten some of the cold lunch they had packed at Remson. He slept under protest, but Frank insisted that after their harrying night trip they both needed sleep. He agreed to take his turn later. In the meantime, in the auto, Billy Barnes and Witherbee dozed off and shared watches with Lathrop and old Mr. Joyce. Neither the miner nor the inventor could drive an auto, so it was necessary to divide up the hours of sleep in this way.

While the lads are taking a rest, it may be as well to turn back to the lone farm at which the *Despatch* party had decided to stop for breakfast. So engrossed had they been over the meal, and so busy had the farm folks been serving them, that none of the party had noticed the boys' aeroplane fly over, and they made very merry at the thought that they were miles ahead of them. Fred Reade was sure they had broken down, and his confidence that they had met with an accident was shared by Luther Barr, Slade and the red-bearded man, whose name was Ethan Aram, and who was Slade's substitute driver.

"I feel like lying down for a nap," said Luther Barr, after breakfast, but his desire was overruled by the others. It was pointed out that he could take a nap in his auto just as well.

"We want to beat those cubs good while we are at it," said Reade, and this stroke of diplomacy won over old Barr. Taking turns at snoozing, therefore, the party pressed on at a leisurely rate, little dreaming that the Boy Aviators were far ahead and nearing Pittsburg. There was another reason for their decreased speed, also. They wished to take advantage of what they considered a great stroke of good luck to let their engine cool off thoroughly.

As the aeroplane flashed above Lockhaven, Pa., the wires began to get red-hot with news of their close approach to Pittsburg. In the Smoky City huge crowds gathered and awaited patiently for hours the coming of the air racers. Every park and open space held its quota of excited people, and flags were run up on every building.

Frank and Harry had both had a sleep before. Pointing to the southwest of their course Harry indicated a heavy dark pall that hung against the sky.

"That must be the Smoky City," he exclaimed, and, sure enough it was. Soon the junction of the Alleghany, Monongahela and Ohio rivers in their Y-shaped formation became visible. Then the dark factory buildings, belching out their clouds of black smoke to make perpetual the city's inky pall. Then the occasional gushes of flame from foundry chimneys, and the long processions of funereal ore and coal barges on the gloomy rivers.

The boys landed in Schenley Park, a fine expanse of wooded and lawned landscape, one of the few beauty spots in the city of gloom. Here it seemed as if at least a quarter of Pittsburg's population was out to greet them. The police had formed hasty lines as soon as it became evident that the boys meant to land on an open stretch of grass, but they had a hard struggle to keep back the crowds. They were speedily re-enforced by reserves from all parts of the city, however, and soon had the crowd in order.

It had been arranged by telegraph that in case of the contestants landing in a public park that the city would allow them to keep the machine there as long as they wanted, so that after the boys had arranged for a guard to be kept over the *Golden Eagle* and the shelter tent carried in the auto—which came chug-chugging up half an hour after the boys had landed—had been rigged, there was nothing to do but to go to the hotel for a wash-up and what Billy Barnes called "a real feed."

Of course the first question the boys had asked when they landed was:

"Anything been seen of the other racers?"

They were delighted to learn that there had not, although they were pretty sure, anyhow, that they were the first to arrive. At the hotel, as the party entered it, having distanced the crowd by speeding through side streets, the manager bustled up and asked for Mr. William Barnes. Billy replied that he was the person sought.

"Then, there's been a wire here for you more than a day," said the manager. "It has been chasing you around every hotel in the city, I guess."

He produced a yellow envelope. Billy opened it eagerly, and then gave a wide grin.

"Whoop-ee, look here," he cried, extending the message to the boys to read.

"Will you accept position special correspondent with aeroplanes for *Planet*? Owe you an apology for unfortunate mistake. Reade's treachery discovered.

"Stowe,
"Managing Editor *Planet*."

Of course Billy Barnes accepted the commission, although for a time he had a struggle with his pride to do so. However, as Frank demonstrated to him, Mr. Stowe had acknowledged his mistake, and he would only have presented himself in the light of a stubborn, obstinate youth if he had refused to accept his offer.

The young reporter was in the Western Union office that night filing a long account of the incidents of the trip, not forgetting the accident to the dirigible and its subsequent safe arrival at Pittsburg — though several hours late — when Fred Reade entered. The Slade aeroplane had descended in Highland Park about three hours after the arrival of the boys, and the chagrin of the *Despatch* people and of Luther Barr and his crowd may be imagined when they learned that they had been badly beaten on the first leg of the trip.

There was a scowl on Reade's face as he sat down and began to write. His anger deepened as he saw that Billy Barnes paid not the slightest attention to him. Finally he said sneeringly:

"What are you writing for now, anyhow? I thought you were out of a job."

"So I was till a short time ago," flashed back Billy, "when the *Planet* seems to have found out something about a young man named Reade."

"What do you mean?" asked Reade in a voice he tried to render blustering, but which shook in spite of himself.

"I'm not going into details; you know well enough," said Billy in a quiet, meaning tone, looking Reade straight in the eye.

The other pretended to get very busy with his writing, but as Billy was leaving the office, he looked up and exclaimed:

"You and your friends think you are mighty smart, but we'll trim you yet, you see if we don't."

"Well, you'll have to wake up, then," laughed Billy, "you didn't do much trimming to-day."

Franke Reade cast a furious glance after the young reporter as he left the telegraph office.

"I'll make you pay for that when we get out in the wild country," he said furiously.

At the hotel Billy found the boys in conversation with McArthur. He had made arrangements to have his ship reinflated that night, he told them, and in future meant to carry with him several cylinders of hydrogen gas. He had telegraphed ahead to Nashville and several other towns on the route to San Francisco to have supplies ready for him, and anticipated no further trouble on that score. He had also been lucky enough to get a propeller from a man who had been making dirigible ascensions at a Pittsburg park, but who had been injured a few days before in an accident.

The boys and their party turned in early and slept like tops. They were up betimes, and after a hasty breakfast motored out to the park. They found the aeroplane in perfect trim, and after replenishing the gasolene and water tanks and thoroughly oiling every part of the engine, they were once more ready to start. A big crowd had gathered, early as was the hour, and gave them a mighty cheer as they swept into the air. The next minute the auto was off, and it was a light-hearted party that occupied its tonneau.

CHAPTER XII. ATTACKED BY COWBOYS.

The Smoky City, with its inky smoke canopy, bluff-bordered rivers and distant heights crowned with beautiful residences, was soon left far behind. But for a long time the boys flew high above veritable gridirons of railroad yards crowded with busy freight trains and puffing yard locomotives. Every one of the engines gave them a screeching greeting as they soared steadily along far above them.

But they were not alone in the air. The Slade machine was close behind them, with his assistant at the wheel. McArthur's dirigible, too, was off a few minutes after the boys took the air. The three racers flew onward with no perceptible difference in the distances between them. Each seemed to be grimly holding its own. At Steubenville, Ohio, the boys struck the Ohio river and flew above its course as far as Ashland, where they crossed the border line of the state into Kentucky.

In forty-eight hours more, having allowed ample time for rests and engine adjustments, they arrived at Nashville, Tenn., having passed the border line of the state a few hours before. For several hours they had not seen the other racers, but at Nashville they learned that Slade's aeroplane had arrived four hours ahead of them, having therefore gained one hour in actual time.

The gain had probably occurred while the boys were delayed at a small town near the Kentucky border fitting new spark plugs, those they used having become badly carbonized by their hard service. They spent little time in the beautiful capital of Tennessee on the banks of the historic Cumberland river. The crowds pestered them to such an extent that they were anxious to hurry on as soon as possible. An examination of the engine, however, showed that it was in need of considerable adjustment, and old Mr. Joyce was compelled to spend several hours over it. The gyroscopic balancer likewise was in need of having its bearings attended to. Slade seemed to have better luck, for his party left Nashville two hours ahead of the Boy Aviators. The start of the *Despatch* craft was closely followed by that of McArthur's dirigible, carrying a large gas supply. The extra weight had been compensated for by ripping out a large part of the cabin and cutting down every ounce carried, so far as it was possible to do so without imperiling the ship.

However, when they finally did take the air from the meadow on the banks of the Cumberland in which they had camped, the boys had the satisfaction of knowing that their craft had had a thorough overhauling. The auto, also, had had new tires fitted and its engine overhauled.

The journey across the rolling plains of Arkansas, skirting the Ozarks to the south, on across the vast levels of Oklahoma, fertile with crops and dotted with thrifty homesteads and small frontier towns, was made without incident. One night the boys found themselves camped on the banks of the Canadian river, not very far from the town of Bravo, in the northwest of the great Panhandle of Texas. For two days, now, they had not seen either of their competitors, and had no idea of where either of them were, though at infrequent opportunities he had in the wild country through which they were now traveling, Billy had tried several times to ascertain by telegraph some word of their whereabouts.

The heat was, as Billy said, enough to fry the horn-toads that crawled about on the vast level that stretched, quivering in the torrid sun rays, as far as the eye could reach on every side of the boys' camping-place. Fortunately they had selected a site beneath an old sycamore tree, which gave them some scanty shade. High against the blazing sky a few turkey-buzzards wheeled, doubtless watching the camps with speculative eyes to ascertain if they were all alive.

But on this latter point there could have existed no doubt in the minds of any human onlookers. The clink-clink of hammers and drills, as the boys worked over their engine with old Mr. Joyce superintending, while Billy Barnes and Lathrop were actively employed loading the auto with a camping kit, gave the camp an appearance of great life and bustle. As for Bart Witherbee, he was at his favorite occupation of cooking. He had shot some young jack-rabbits a few hours before, and was now composing a stew.

"I didn't know jack-rabbits were good to eat," exclaimed Billy, when the miner had brought them into camp.

"Young ones is," explained the plainsman, "but keep away from the elderly jack-rabbits."

Suddenly Billy, who had looked from his task for the fiftieth time to remark that it was hot, noticed quite a cloud of dust swirling toward the adventurers across the prairie.

"Gee, here comes a whirlwind!" he exclaimed, pointing. The others looked, too.

"Maybe it's a cyclone," suggested Harry.

Old Witherbee placed his hand over his eyebrows and peered long and earnestly at the rapidly approaching cloud of yellow dust.

"Whatever is it?" asked Frank.

"Somethin' that I'm afeard is goin' ter make it mighty uncomfortable for us," exclaimed Witherbee, with a tone of anxiety in his voice.

"Mighty uncomfortable, how? Will it blow the auto away?" asked Billy.

"No, youngster, but it may blow us up; that cloud yonder is a bunch of skylarking cowboys, and they're coming right for us."

"Will they kill us?" asked Billy anxiously.

"No, I don't think it'll be as bad as that; though they git mighty onery sometimes. Don't you boys give 'em no back talk, and maybe we'll get out all right."

The rapid advance of the approaching cowboys could now be heard. Their ponies' hoofs could also be seen as they flashed in and out under the cloud of dust.

Suddenly there was a terrific volley of yells, and, as the cavalcade drew rein, the cloud rolled away and the boys found they were surrounded by forty or fifty wild-looking fellows, all yelling and shouting. Some of them had revolvers and were firing them in the air. The din was terrific.

"Throw up yer hands, yer Scanderhovian bunch of tenderfeet," shouted the leader, a big man on a buckskin pony, whose legs were incased, despite the intense heat, in a huge, hairy pair of bearskin "chaps."

The boys all elevated their hands, and old man Joyce and Bart Witherbee hastened to follow their example.

"Where's this yar sky schooner yer goin' a-sailin' around in, scaring our cattle and driving the critters plumb crazy?" he demanded angrily.

"If you mean our aeroplane, there it is," said Frank, indicating the machine.

"Wall, there was two of them went over here yesterday, and all the beef critters on the Bar X range is plum stampeded all over the per-arie. We're goin' ter stop this, an' we might as well begin right now. Come on, boys, shoot the blame thing full o' holes and put a few in ther choo-choo wagin while yer at it."

The situation was critical indeed.

The boys saw no way of saving their aeroplane, and to add to their troubles they had been informed that their two rivals were in front of them.

Frank alone retained his presence of mind. He saw that only by a trick could they regain their safety from the desperate men into whose power they had fallen.

"Did you ever see an aeroplane before?" he asked of the leader.

"No, I never did," replied the other; "why?"

"Well, you seem to have a pretty dry part of the country out here, and I guess a little rain would do it no harm."

"That's right, stranger, you never spoke a truer word; but what in thunder has that got to do with yer blamed scaryplane, or whatever you call it, scaring all our beef critters away?"

"I am very sorry for your misfortune, Mr. — Mr. — —"

"Rattlesnake Ike is my name, with no blame 'Mister' on it, young tenderfoot," growled the other.

"Well, Rattlesnake Ike, we can make rain."

"What?" roared the whole assemblage.

"We can make rain," calmly repeated the boy, "with that aeroplane."

"Wall, now, stranger, how kin yer do that—tell us," demanded the leader of the cowboys, leaning forward on the bow of his saddle, deeply interested.

"Well, you've heard that explosions near the sky will concentrate the moisture, thus causing it to condense in a copious rainfall," declaimed Frank pompously, putting in all the long words he could think of.

"Hump—wall," dubiously remarked the cowboy, scratching his head, "I dunno as I hev, but you seem ter have it all down pat."

"That's what we've been doing with our aeroplane," went on Frank, "making rain. Haven't we?" he turned to Witherbee questioningly. The miner at once saw what he was driving at.

"Sure," said the old miner. "Why, pardners, down in Arkansaw they had forgotten what rain looked like till we came along. We made it pour for three days."

"And that scaryplane does it?"

"Well, we go up in it and then fire bombs from this rain-gun."

Frank indicated the searchlight as he spoke.

"Wall, I'd sure like ter see that," said the leader. "How about it, boys?"

"Let's see what they kin do; but if yer don't make it rain, strangers, we'll string you all up ter that sycamore tree," decided one of the group.

They all chorused assent, and Frank and Harry at once got into the machine.

"Hand me some rain bombs, Billy," said Frank.

Billy Barnes reached into the tonneau and produced some blue flares. These he handed to Frank.

"Take care they don't go off, Frank," he said solemnly.

"Yes; you recollect them twenty fellers as was killed in St. Looey," warned old Witherbee solemnly.

"Say, strangers, are them there things dangerous?" asked the cowboy leader.

"Well, there's enough dynamite in them to blow that river there clean into the next county," rejoined Frank, "but don't be scared, we won't drop them."

"Get into the auto when we are well up," Frank whispered rapidly to Billy, while the cowboys exchanged awed glances.

"Now, gentlemen," he went on aloud, "get your umbrellas ready, for pretty soon there's going to be some big rain."

The aeroplane started up while the cowboys yelled and whooped. It had reached a height of about two hundred feet, and was circling above their heads, when Harry suddenly lighted one of the fizzing blue flares; at the same instant Billy, followed by the others, leaped into the auto.

"Hey, stop that!" yelled the cowboy leader, but at the same moment he broke off with a yell of terror.

"Look out for the dynamite bomb!" yelled Harry, as he dropped the flaming blue flare over the side of the aeroplane, fairly on top of the gang of cowboys.

"Ride for your lives, boys!" shouted the leader of the cowboys, as the flaming light dropped, "she's goin' ter bust."

They didn't need any urging, but fled with wild cries.

By the time the cattlemen realized they had been tricked, the auto was away on the prairie, speeding on toward the west in a cloud of dust, while the aeroplane was far out of range.

CHAPTER XIII. INDIANS!

"Ah, now we are beginning to get into my own country again; this begins ter look like home," exclaimed Bart Witherbee, one day as the adventurers made camp in a canyon in one of the southernmost spurs of the Rockies in the state of New Mexico. The boys had made the detour to the south to avoid crossing the range itself, which would have been a difficult, if not an impossible, task in an aeroplane.

Still they had not sighted the rival racing air-craft, but they knew that the others could not be far ahead now, as at a small settlement they stopped at the day before they learned that the Slade party had called at the blacksmith shop there to repair a truss brace that had snapped. As the facilities of the smithy were rather clumsy for the fine work that has to be done on the aeroplane, the Slade machine was delayed several hours. So far as their judgment went, the boys decided that the other party could not be much more than fifty miles ahead of them.

As for the dirigible, they had heard that the expansion of its gas bag, caused by the sun, had compelled it to remain all one day in a small town in the Texas Panhandle, and that while it was journeying across the arid country it could travel only short distances. The boys, therefore, felt much cheered as at sundown they alighted by the side of a brawling mountain stream and made camp. Bart Witherbee at once got out his improvised fishing tackle and started up the stream in search of trout, which he declared would abound in such waters.

"We'll have a change from canned beef, canned soup and canned vegetables to-night, boys," he declared, "if I haven't lost the knack of it."

They listened to his heavy footsteps plunging up the steep hillside till they died out, and then took up the ordinary occupations of the camp. The rocky defile up which the old miner had disappeared on his quest was well covered with pine timber almost down to where it reached the arid ground on the edge of which the lads were camped. Except for the occasional scream of a hawk making for its night roost, or the crash of some animal making its way through the dense growth that grew higher up on the hillside, the place was as quiet as a cemetery.

Billy Barnes was examining his camera, which had been severely shaken up on the trip, Frank and Harry were going over the *Golden Eagle* admiringly, remarking on the way she had stood her hard ordeal, and old Mr. Joyce was taking a lesson in wireless telegraphy from Lathrop. It was beginning to grow dusk. Somewhere far up on the hillside there came the hoot of an owl. The hush of the evening in the foothills lay over everything, when suddenly the silence was broken by a sound that brought them all to their feet.

The report of a rifle had rung out on the hillside above them.

"Must be Bart shooting at something," remarked Billy, gazing at the scared faces about him.

"That was a rifle shot," said Frank slowly, "and Bart Witherbee carried no rifle."

"Then somebody else fired it?"

"That's about it. Don't make a sound now. Listen!"

They all held their breaths and waited anxiously in the stillness that followed. For perhaps ten minutes they stood so, and then there came a sharp crackle of snapping twigs, that told them some one was descending the hillside.

Who was it?

Several minutes of agonizing suspense followed before they knew whether it was friend or enemy advancing toward them. Then Bart Witherbee glided, like a snake, out of the woods.

"What's the mat— —" began Frank. But he checked himself instantly.

Bart Witherbee's hand was held up.

Every one of the group read that mute signal aright.

Silence!

The old plainsman waited till he got right up to the group before he spoke, and then it was in a hushed tense whisper.

"Injuns," he said, "they're up on the hillside."

"How many?" whispered back Frank.

"I dunno exactly, after that there bullet I didn't wait ter see, and say, boys, I had ter leave as nice a string of trout as you ever see up there fer them pesky redskins ter git at."

"Never mind the fish, Bart," urged Frank, "tell us, is there danger?"

"There's allus danger when Injuns is aroun', and think they kin git somethin' that's vallerble without gitting in trouble over it," was the westerner's reply.

"We'd better get away from here right away," exclaimed Harry.

"Not on your life, son," was Bart's reply; "not if I know anything about Injuns an' their ways. No, sons, my advice is ter git riddy fer 'em. They was startled when they see me, therefore they didn't know we wus here till they stumbled on me. That bein' the case, I reckin they don't know about that thar flying thing of you boys."

"And you think we can scare them with it?" began Frank eagerly.

"Not so fast, son, not so fast," reprimanded the old man. "Now, them Injuns won't attack afore dark, if they do at all. An' when they do, they'll come frum up the mountain-side. Now, my idee is to git that thar searchlight o' yours rigged up, and hev it handy, so as when we hear a twig crack we kin switch it on and pick 'em out at our leisure."

"That's a fine idea, Bart, but what if they attack us from behind?" suggested Frank.

"They won't do that. Yer see, behind us it's all open country. Wall, Injuns like plenty of cover when they fight."

"Perhaps we could connect up some blue flares, and plant them on rocks up the hillside, and scare them that way," suggested Billy.

"That's a good idee, son, but who's goin' ter go up there an' light 'em? It would be certain death."

"Nobody would have to go up and light them," eagerly put in Harry. "We can wire them up and then just touch them off when we are ready. We can get plenty of spark by connecting up all our batteries."

"Wall, now, that's fine and dandy," exclaimed the miner admiringly, "see what it is ter hev an eddercation. Wall, boys, if we're goin' ter do that, now's the time. Them Injuns won't attack afore dark, and if we want ter git ready we'd better do it now."

While Frank and Harry planted the blue flares on rocks on the hillside within easy range of the camp, and old Mr. Joyce utilized his electrical skill in wiring them up and connecting them to a common switch, Billy and Lathrop and Bart Witherbee struck camp and packed the paraphernalia in the tonneau of the auto.

"Better be ready ter make a quick gitaway," was the miner's recommendation.

These tasks completed, there was nothing to do but to wait for a sign of the attack. This was nervous work. Bart had informed the boys that in his opinion the Indians were a band from a reservation not many miles from there who had somehow got hold of a lot of "firewater" and had "got bad."

"I'll bet yer there's troops after 'em now, if we did but know it," he opined.

"Well, I wish the troops would get here quick," bemoaned Harry.

"They won't git here in time ter be of much use ter us," remarked old Bart, grimly biting off a big chew of tobacco, "and now, boys, keep quiet, and mind, don't fire till I tell yer, and don't switch on them lights till I give you the word."

How long they waited neither Frank nor Harry nor any of the others could ever tell, but it seemed to be years before there came a sudden owl hoot far up on the hillside.

"Here they come, that's their signal," whispered old Bart in Frank's ear; "steady now."

"I'm all right," replied Frank, as calmly as he could, though his heart beat wildly.

The hoot was answered by another one, and then all was silence.

Suddenly there came the crack of a twig somewhere above. It was only a mite of a noise, but in the stillness it sounded as startling as a pistol shot.

"We won't have to wait long now," commented Bart in a tense undertone; "all ready, now."

Each of the boys gripped his rifle determinedly. Old Mr. Joyce had been armed with a pistol. At their elbows lay their magazine revolvers fully loaded.

Following the first snapping of the twig there was a long interval of silence. Then the staccato rattle of a small dislodged rock bounding down the hillside set all hearts to beating once more.

The attack was evidently not to be delayed many moments now.

It came with the suddenness of the bursting of a tropical storm.

Hardly had the boys drawn their breath following the breathless suspense that ensued on the falling of the rock before there was a wild yell, and half a dozen dark forms burst out of the trees. They were received with a fusillade, but none of them were hurt, as they all vanished almost as quickly as they had appeared.

"That was just to see if we was on the lookout," said old Bart in a whisper. "I reckon they found we was. Look out for the next attack."

They hadn't long to wait. There was a rattle of falling stones as the main body rushed down the hillside.

"*Now!*"

Old Bart fairly screamed the command in his excitement.

At the same instant Billy shoved over the switch that connected the sparking wires of the blue-flare battery with the electric supply for the wireless, and the whole woodland was instantly illumined as if by the most brilliant moonlight.

With cries and yells of amazement, a score of the attacking redskins wheeled and vanished into the dark shadows of the hillside. The lights glared up, brilliantly illuminating everything in the vicinity, but the Indians were far too scared to come out of their hiding-place and renew the attack.

"Fire a volley up the hillside," ordered Bart. "We can't hit any of 'em, but it will add to their scare and keep 'em off till I can work out a plan."

There was a rattling discharge of shots, which met with no return, and then, as the lights began to burn dimly Bart ordered Frank and Harry to get into the aeroplane and sail into the air.

"Turn your searchlight on the wood from up above, and they'll run from here to San Franciskey," he declared.

Though rather dubious of the success of the experiment, the boys obeyed, and in a few seconds the roaring drone of the engine was heard far above the wood, while the great eye of the searchlight seemed to penetrate into its darkest depths.

If the boys had had any doubt as to the feasibility of Bart's recipe for scaring Indians they regained their faith then and there. With yells that echoed into the night, the redskins ran for their lives, tumbling over each other in their hurry to escape the "Air Devil."

What the blue lights had begun the aeroplane had completed.

"It's goin' ter take a year ter round them fellers up ag'in," commented Bart.

CHAPTER XIV. THE AUTO IN DIFFICULTIES.

As Bart had expected, the boys were troubled no more that night, although there was naturally little enough sleep for any one. It was soon after daybreak and they were at breakfast when, across the plain, at the foot of the spur on which they were encamped, the boys saw a detachment of horsemen riding rapidly toward them. Through the glasses the boys speedily made them out as United States cavalrymen. They were advancing at a smart trot, and soon reached the boys' camp.

"Good-morning," said the officer at their head, "you seem to be breakfasting quietly enough, but you might not be taking it so easy if I were to tell you that several Indians have gone off the reservation and have managed to secure enough bad whiskey to make them very dangerous."

"I guess, captain, that we had a bit of a run-in with your Indians last night," said Frank, with a quiet smile.

"What? Why, God bless my soul, they are very bad men; it's a wonder any of you are alive. How did it happen?"

Frank detailed the happenings of the night, being frequently interrupted by the officer's exclamations of amazement. He regretted, though, that they had been so badly scared, as he anticipated a long journey before he crossed their trail again.

The attention of the captain and his troopers was then attracted by the aeroplane. They had read in the papers that found their way to the lone desert post of the great flight, and were much interested in the boys' story of their adventure. The officer told them that he, himself, was much interested in aerial navigation and had constructed several experimental craft. He expected, he said, to be detailed by the government before very long to undertake an important expedition. His ambition was to reach the South Pole, just as his fellow officer, Commander Peary, attained the northernmost pinnacle of the earth.

After a little more conversation, the officer, who said his name was Captain Robert Hazzard, and the boys parted with many warm expressions of friendship. The whole company of troopers, however, waited till the aeroplane had soared into the air, and the auto chugged off beneath it, before they wheeled their wiry little horses and started off on the long weary chase after the Indians.

As the boys in the auto spun along over the level expanse of prairie, which, except where the rough road traversed it, was overgrown with sage-brush and cactus plants, the car came to a sudden stop. Then, without any warning, it plunged forward and seemed to drop quite a few feet.

Billy, who was driving, instantly shut off power, and gazed back in amazement. The auto was sunk to its hubs in mud. There was no doubt about it. The substance in which it was stuck was unmistakable mud.

"It's a mud hole," exclaimed Bart Witherbee; "now we are stuck with a vengeance."

"But what on earth is mud doing out in the middle of a dry desert?" demanded Lathrop.

"I dunno how it gits thar; no one does," responded Bart; "maybe its hidden springs or something, but every year cattle git lost that way. They are walking over what seemed solid ground when the crust breaks, and bang! down they go, just like us."

"But this is a trail," objected Billy, "wagons must go over it."

"No wagons as heavy as this yer chuck cart, I guess," was Bart's reply.

"We must signal the *Golden Eagle* of our plight," was Lathrop's exclamation.

"But the wireless mast is down," objected Billy; "we can't."

"Consarn it, that's so," agreed Bart. "Well, we've got to signal 'em somehow. Let's fire our pistols."

The *Golden Eagle* seemed quite a distance off, but the lads got out their revolvers and fired a fusillade. However, if they had but known it, there was no need for them to have wasted ammunition, for Harry, through his glasses, had already seen that something was wrong with their convoy.

The aeroplane at once turned back, and was soon on the plain alongside the boys. By this time they had all got out and were busy dragging all the heavy articles from the tonneau so as to lighten it as much as possible. A long rope was then attached to the front axle and they all heaved with all their might. The auto did not budge an inch, however.

In fact, it seemed to be sinking more deeply in the mud.

"We've got to do something and do it quick," declared Bart, "if we don't, the mud hole may swallow our gasolene gig, and then we'd die of thirst afore we could reach a settlement."

They desperately tugged and heaved once more, but their efforts were of no avail.

"I've got an idea," suddenly exclaimed Frank; "maybe if we hitch the *Golden Eagle* to the rope it will help."

"It's worth trying, and we've got to do something," agreed Bart. "Come on, then. Couple up."

The rope was attached to the lower frame of the *Golden Eagle*, and while they all hauled Frank started up the engine of the aeroplane. For a second or so the propellers of the *Golden Eagle* beat the air without result, then suddenly the boys' throats were rent with a loud "Hurrah," as the auto budged a tiny bit. Not far from the trail were the ruins of an old hut. Several stout beams were still standing upright amid the debris.

"Hold on a bit," shouted Bart suddenly.

He seized up an axe from the heap of camp kit that had been hastily thrown on the ground and started for the ruins. In a few minutes he was back with four stout levers.

By using these, they managed to raise the auto still more, and wedge the wheels under with other bits of timber obtained from the demolished hut.

Then the aeroplane was started up once more, and this time the auto, with a loud cheer, was dragged clear of the treacherous hole.

"We'll just stick up a bit of timber here to warn any one else that comes along," declared Bart, as he fixed a tall timber in the ground where it would attract the attention of any traveler coming along the road.

Soon after this, a start was made, and the aeroplane and the auto made good time across the blazing hot plain. All the afternoon they traveled until Billy Barnes fairly cried out for a stop.

"I'm so thirsty I could die," he declared.

"Then get a drink," recommended Bart Witherbee, indicating the zinc water tank under the tonneau seat.

"It's empty," said Lathrop. "I tried it a little while ago."

"Empty," echoed Witherbee, his face growing grave. "Here, let's have a look at that map, youngster, and see where's our next watering place."

Billy Barnes, with a look of comical despair, handed it over. "I'll have to wait for a drink of water till we get to a town, I suppose. What do you want the map for, Bart?"

"Fer that very reason—ter see how soon we do get to a town. I'd like a drink myself just about now."

He perused the map for a minute in silence. Then he looked up, his face graver even than before.

"Well, she can go sixty miles or better, but I'm afraid of heating the engine too much if we travel at that pace," responded Billy, who was at the steering wheel.

"Well, we've got to hustle; it's most a hundred miles to Gitalong, and that's the nearest town to us."

"Nonsense, Bart," exclaimed Lathrop, pointing to another name on the wide waste, which on the map represents sparsely settled New Mexico, "here's a place called Cow Wells."

"No, thar ain't," was Bart's reply.

"There isn't?"

"No."

"But here it is on the map."

"That's all right; maps ain't always ter be relied on any more than preachers. Cow Wells has gone dry. I reckon that's why they called it Cow Wells. Everybody has moved away. It used ter be a mining camp."

"Are you sure it's abandoned?" asked Billy in a trembling voice.

"Sartain sure," responded Bart. "I heard about it when I come through on my way east."

"Then we can't get a thing to drink till we reach Gitalong?"

"That's about the size of it," was the dispiriting reply of the old plainsman.

CHAPTER XV. THIRST — AND A PLOT.

While the lads in the auto were thus discussing the doleful prospect ahead of them, Frank and Harry were making good time through the upper air on the run toward Cow Wells, which they had noted on their maps as the spot by which they would stop for refreshment. As they neared it in due time, from a distance of a mile away they noted its desolate appearance.

"There doesn't seem to be much of anything there," remarked Frank, as he looked ahead of him at the collection of ramshackle buildings that they knew from their observations must be Cow Wells.

"I don't see a soul moving," declared Harry.

"Neither do I," was the other lad's response. "Maybe they are all away at a festival or something."

"Well, we'll get water there, anyhow," remarked Frank. "I'm so thirsty I could drink a river dry."

"Same here."

As the boys neared it, the lifeless appearance of Cow Wells became even more marked. The timbers of the houses had baked a dirty gray color in the hot sun, and what few buildings had been painted had all faded to the same neutral hue. The pigment had peeled off them under the heat in huge patches.

Of all the towns the boys had so far encountered on their transcontinental trip, this was the first one, however small, in which there had not been a rush of eager inhabitants to see the wonderful aeroplane.

"They must be all asleep," laughed Harry; "here, we'll wake them up."

He drew his revolver and fired a volley of shots.

For reply, instead of a rush of startled townsfolk, a gray coyote silently slipped from a ruined barn and slunk across the prairie.

The truth burst on both the boys at once.

"The place is deserted," exclaimed Harry.

"We can get some water there though, I guess, just the same," replied the other. "There must be some wells left."

They swooped down onto the silent, deserted town, in which the sand had drifted high in front of many of the houses. Eagerly they climbed out of the chassis of the aeroplane and investigated the place.

"Hurray," suddenly shouted Harry, rushing up to a large building with a long porch, that had evidently once been the hotel, "here's a pump."

He pointed to an aged iron pump that stood in front of the tumbled down building. But the boys were doomed once more to disappointment. A few strokes of its clanking handle showed them that it was a long time since water had passed its spout. They investigated other wells with the same result.

The boys exchanged blank looks as they realized that they were to get no water there, but suddenly the realization that the auto was back there in the desert somewhere with a tank full of water cheered them.

"They've lots of water in the tank," suggested Harry.

"I guess that's right; we'd better wait till they come and get a drink of it. I'd almost give my chances in the race for a big glass of lemonade right now."

"Don't talk of such things, you only make it worse," groaned Harry. "Just plain ice water would do me fine. I could drink a whole cooler full of it."

"Same here—but listen—here comes the auto."

Sure enough the chug-chug of their escort was drawing near down the rough desert road.

"Say, fellows," shouted both boys, as the auto rolled up, "how about a drink of water from the tank?"

"Gee whiz," groaned Billy, "that's just the trouble. There's not a drop in it."

"What, no water?" exclaimed Frank blankly.

"Not a drop, and Bart says we can't get any here."

"That's right; we've investigated."

"What are we going to do?"

"Keep on to Gitalong, that's the thing to do. If you don't get there within half an hour of our arrival we'll start out after you with water."

"I suppose that's all we can do," groaned poor Billy.

"And the quicker we do it, the better," briskly announced Frank. "Come on, Harry; ho for Gitalong, and to the dickens with Cow Wells, where there are no cows and no wells."

"That's why they gave it the name, I guess," commented Lathrop, with a sorrowful grin.

It grew hotter and hotter as the afternoon wore on. Billy finally, although he stuck to the wheel pluckily as long as he was able, was compelled to give it up to Lathrop. After that he lay on the floor of the tonneau, suffering terrible torments from his raging thirst.

Old Bart sat grimly by Lathrop's side, encouraging him as well as he knew how, and the boy bravely smiled at the old miner's jokes and stories, although each smile made his parched lips crack.

"Why, what's the matter?" remarked Lathrop suddenly, as the auto seemed to slow down and come to a stop of itself.

"I dunno; you're an auto driver, you ought to know," said Bart.

"The engine's overheated," pronounced old man Joyce. "Look at the steam coming from the cap of the radiator."

He pointed to a slender wisp of white vapor. It indicated to Lathrop at once that Mr. Joyce was right. The accident they had dreaded had happened. It might be hours before they could proceed.

"What can we do?" demanded Bart Witherbee.

"Nothing," responded Lathrop, "except to let her cool off. The cylinders have jammed, and the metal won't cool sufficiently till the evening to allow us to proceed."

"We're stuck here, then?"

"That's it, Bart. We had better crawl under the machine. We shall get some shade there, anyhow."

"A good idee, youngster; come on, Mr. Joyce. Here, Lathrop, bear a hand here, and help me get poor Billy out."

The fleshy young reporter was indeed in a sad state. His stoutness made the heat harder for him to bear than the others. They rolled him into the shade under the auto and there they all lay till sundown, panting painfully. As the sun dropped it grew cooler, and gradually a slight breeze crept over the burning waste. As it did so the adventurers crawled from their retreat, even Billy partially reviving in the grateful drop in the temperature. But there was still no sign of the aeroplane.

After a brief examination of the engine Lathrop announced that the party could proceed, and he started up the engine cautiously. It seemed to work all right, and once more the auto moved forward. They had not proceeded more than two miles when they heard a shout in the air over their heads, and there was the *Golden Eagle* circling not far above them.

Lathrop instantly stopped the machine, and the aeroplane swept down. Frank and Harry had brought with them a plentiful supply of water in canteens.

The boys drank as if they would never stop.

"I never tasted an ice-cream soda as good," declared Billy.

Refreshed and invigorated, the adventurers resumed their journey toward Gitalong as soon as they had fully quenched their thirst, and poured some of the water over their sun-parched faces and hands. They reached the town late in the evening and were warmly welcomed by the citizens, mostly cowboys and Indians, who had sat up to await their arrival. Several of them, in fact, rode far out onto the prairie and, with popping revolvers and loud yells, escorted the auto party into town.

The aeroplane was stored in a livery stable that night, while the boys registered at the Lucky Strike hotel. The Lucky Strike's menu was mostly beans, but they made a good meal. They had hardly got into their beds, which were all placed in a long room, right under the rafters, when they heard to their amazement the sound of an auto approaching the place. It drew up in front of the hotel and the listeners heard heavy steps as its occupants climbed out of it and entered the bar.

They called for drinks in loud tones, and then demanded to see a man they called Wild Bill Jenkins.

"Why, Wild Bill Jenkins is just sitting in a friendly game o' monte," the boys could hear the bartender reply, "but if it's anything very partic'lar I'll call him, though he'll rile up rough at bein' disturbed."

"Yes, it is very particular," piped up another voice, evidently that of one of the automobile arrivals; "we must see him at once."

The boys, with a start, recognized the voice of the speaker as that of Luther Barr.

"Must hev come quite a way in that buzz wagon of yours, stranger," volunteered the bartender.

"Yes, we've driven over from Pintoville — it's a good twenty miles, I should say."

"Wall, we don't call that more than a step out here," rejoined the man who presided over the Lucky Strike's bar.

In the meantime a messenger had been despatched to summon Wild Bill Jenkins. Pretty soon he came. He was in a bad temper over being interrupted at his game apparently.

"Who is the gasolene gig-riders as disturbed Wild Bill Jenkins at his game?" he roared. "Show 'em to me, an' I'll fill 'em so full of lead they'll be worth a nickel a pound."

"That will do, Bill," put in another voice, seemingly Hank Higgins.

Wild Bill Jenkins' manner instantly changed.

"Why, hello. Hank Higgins!" he exclaimed, "hullo, Noggy Wilkes. Air you in company with this old coyote?"

"Hush, Bill; that is Mr. Luther Barr, a very wealthy gentleman, and he wants to put you in the way of making a bit of money."

"Oh, he does, does he? Wall, here's my paw, stranger. Money always looks good to Bill Jenkins, and he'll do most anything to get it."

"This will be an easy task," rejoined Luther Barr. "All you have to do is to tell us the location of that mine you know about. I will buy it from you. But we must be quick, for others are in search of it—Bart Witherbee and some boys that call themselves the Boy Aviators."

"Why, that's the bunch that came in here to-night," exclaimed Wild Bill Jenkins.

"It is?"

"They are here now."

"Are you sure of that?"

"Sure."

"Where?"

"Right here in this hotel. I guess they're asleep in their little cots now, right over your heads."

"You don't think it possible that they can have heard any of our conversation?"

"Not on your natural, stranger. We're as safe talking here as in the Alloff Gastorium in New York. Is that all you want me to do?"

"That's all. I will pay you well for the information when you deliver the map to me."

"I'll deliver it, never fear. It was a lucky day for me I stumbled on that old mine. I've never been able to claim it, though, for they'd lynch me for a little shooting if I showed my face there."

"Those cubs have made good time. We are only twenty miles ahead of them," struck in another voice—that of Fred Reade; "if we could only disable their machine it would come near putting them out of the race."

"What, bust their fool sky wagon. That's easy enough," said Wild Bill Jenkins confidently. "Listen here."

But some other customers entered the bar at this point, and the plotters sank their tones so low that the boys could hear no more.

CHAPTER XVI. THE AUTO GONE.

"Harry!"

"What is it, Frank?"

"Get on your clothes. You, too, Bart Witherbee, and be sure to conceal the map of your mine carefully."

"What be yer goin' ter do, Frank?"

"Fool those rascals. There is no doubt they are going to the stable and try to disable our aeroplane."

"I reckon we'll fool 'em, Frank."

"I hope so. We must make haste. Come on out through this window here. It leads onto a back porch. We can slip down a support without anyone seeing us and get round to the stable before they get up from their table. They'll be in no hurry, for they think we're asleep."

"What are we to do, Frank?" asked Billy Barnes and Lathrop, who, with old Mr. Joyce, were evidently to be left behind.

"Just snore as loud as ever you can. There is no doubt that they will creep up here after a while to see if we are asleep. If they hear you snoring they will think everything is all right."

Frank, Harry and their hard companion were soon out of the window and on the ground. They found themselves on a back street, or rather, a mere trail on the prairie, for the town consisted of but a single street. They rapidly made their way to the livery stable. The man who owned it was there, and at first was inclined to be angry at being awakened.

He appeared at his door with a gun.

"Git out of here, you no good drunken cattle rustlers," he bellowed, "or I'll fill you full of lead. Don't come skylarking around me."

96

"We are not cattle rustlers. We're the boys who own that aeroplane," explained Frank. "We heard to-night, or rather we overheard, a plot to damage it so that it could not win the race."

"What's that?" demanded the other, "some no good, ornery cusses undertook ter come roun't here and do up that thar contraption of yourn?"

"That's it."

"Wall, I don't know as I'd blame anyone fer wantin' ter bust up such things. Hosses air good enough fer us out here in the west, but nobody ain't goin' to hurt nothin' of nobody's while it's under my care. Come on in an' tell me about it."

The boys' story was soon told. When it was concluded the stable man was mad clear through.

"What, that hobo of a Wild Bill Jenkins, as he calls his self, come aroun' here and try monkey tricks in my barn? Not much," he kept repeating. "Hev you boys got shootin'-irons?"

"We shore have," replied old Bart Witherbee.

"Well, you at least look like a party as could use one," remarked the stable man, gazing at Bart's rugged face. "Now the only thing to do is to wait for them to come."

"That's it, I guess," agreed Frank. "They can't be so very long if they want to get away before daylight."

But the boys little knew the ingenious plan that the rogues had decided on to compass their ends and destroy the *Golden Eagle*. Even while they sat there waiting Luther Barr and the others were working out their scheme.

Before long there was the distant chug-chug of an auto heard and as the machine drove away, the sound diminished till it died out.

"Well, I guess your friends decided that they'd put their little expedition off," grinned the stable keeper. "There they go and good riddance to 'em, I say."

They waited a while longer, but there was no demonstration of their enemies' presence. Suddenly Frank sniffed curiously.

"Do you smell anything?" he asked presently. "It seems to me there's something burning somewhere."

"I noticed it, too," said Harry.

At the same instant there was a glare of red flame from the rear of the stable.

"Fire!" shouted the stableman.

His cry rang through the night, and in a few seconds the small prairie town was ringing with it. The flames gained rapid headway. They ate through the sun-dried timbers of the stable as if it had been made of paper.

The stableman and his friends rushed madly about getting out horses and rigs to places of safety. As for the boys and Bart they seized hold of the aeroplane and dragged it beyond reach of the flames. They then ran out the auto. This done they returned and helped the stableman. Soon all the stock and valuable buggies were out of the place and it was a roaring mass of savage flames. There was no fire department in Gitalong, so the inhabitants, instead of wasting their efforts on trying to extinguish the blaze with buckets of water, devoted their attention to wetting down adjoining roofs in order to prevent the flames spreading. The boys were so busy attending to this work that they didn't stop to notice what had become of their companions. They had had, however, a moment to exchange a hasty word with Billy, Lathrop and old man Joyce, who had hastened from the hotel at the first cry of alarm.

The flames were about out and the barn was reduced to a smouldering heap of ashes before they had time to look about them.

"Why, where's Mr. Joyce?" suddenly exclaimed Bart.

"He was here a minute ago," rejoined Frank. "Have you seen him, Billy?"

"Not for the last ten minutes," replied the other. "What can have become of him?"

"I guess he got tired and went back to the hotel," suggested Harry.

"That must be it. Come on, let's go and see if he is all right."

They started off, but on the way were halted by the stableman.

"Thank you, boys, for helping me!" he exclaimed warmly, extending his hand. "It was mighty white of you."

"I hope your loss was not very heavy," said Frank.

"Oh, no; I had that covered by insurance. A good thing I had, too. If ever I get my hands on that rascal, Wild Bill Jenkins, I'll make it hot for him."

"Why; do you suspect him of setting it?"

"Not only him but your friends — or whatever you like to call 'em. The scalliwags suspected we might be on the lookout for 'em, and so we were, but at the wrong door. While we were expecting 'em to come sneaking up in front they walks up behind and sets a fire. They'd fix your aeroplane forever and a day, they thought, and as for my barn they didn't bother about that."

"That must be it," exclaimed Frank. "I'd like to get my hands on the rascals."

"Let's drive after them and have them arrested at Pintoville. We can easily do it," suggested Billy.

"All right, you and Bart take the auto. I've got to find Mr. Joyce."

"*Where is the auto?*" suddenly exclaimed Harry, looking about him. "It was here while we were working at the fire and now it's gone."

"Gone!" gasped the others.

"Yes, gone. Look, there's not a sign of it."

"That's right," said the stableman; "looks like that chu-chu cart had flown away. Wall, if it's in this town it won't take long to find it."

The stableman, who the boys now found out was also mayor, at once ordered out several men with instructions to search for the missing car, but they all reported half an hour later, when the town had been thoroughly searched, that not a trace of it could be found.

In the meantime a search had been conducted for old Mr. Joyce, but he also had vanished as mysteriously as the auto.

"What can have become of them?" exclaimed Frank, despairingly. "Without the auto and our supplies we cannot go any further."

At this juncture a man came rushing up with a report that searchers had found the tracks of two autos, both going out of the town over the Pintoville road.

"Pintoville is where Luther Barr is staying," cried Frank.

"Then you can depend upon it," rejoined their friend, the mayor, "that that is where your auto and the old man have gone."

"But why should they want to kidnap old Mr. Joyce?" demanded Frank.

"You'll have to ask me an easy one," answered the mayor, picking up a straw and sucking it with deep meditation.

CHAPTER XVII. THE WRONG MAN.

In the meantime, while the glare of the flames still shone behind them, two autos were speeding over the plains. The first, in which was seated Luther Barr, Frank Reade and Hank Higgins, had been waiting just outside the town ever since the boys had heard it chug away before the fire started.

Barr and his companions had spent the interim in ill-disguised impatience. Reade in particular seemed gloomy and apprehensive.

"This is dangerous business, Barr," he said. "If anything falls through, we might as well make up our minds to be lynched."

"What is the use of talking like that," snapped the old man. "Wild Bill Jenkins is a reliable man, Hank."

"He sure is that, Barr," rejoined the gambler. "If he says he'll do a thing that thing is as good as did, and you may take your gospel on that."

"And your partner, Noggy Wilkes?"

"Why, Barr," declared the other earnestly, "that feller would rather stick up a stage or rob a bank than sit down to a chicken dinner."

"Hum," said old Barr, evidently highly pleased by the very dubious recommendations, "he must be an enterprising young man."

"I don't know what that ther word may mean, Barr," declared Higgins, gravely, "but if et means he's a good man for this job you can take your Davy he is."

"I wish they would hurry up and start in," the old man began again, after an interval of silence; "they take a long time getting to work."

"Well, you know this isn't a job to be hurried," declared Hank.

"No, indeed," stammered Frank Reade nervously, "it's better to do it safely and have no blunders. If it was found out that we had attempted such a thing it would be our ruin. What will we do with Witherbee when we get him?"

"Drop him down a shaft some place; we want to be sure he doesn't follow us to the mine," said Hank.

The occupants of the touring car were silent for a time, and then suddenly old Barr held up a finger.

"Hark!" he exclaimed.

Very faintly the uproar that accompanied the outbreak of the fire was borne to their ears.

Suddenly a brisk little puff of the night wind of the prairie blew toward them. On its wings were borne the cry for which they had been waiting:

"Fire! Fire! Fire!"

"They've done it," grinned old Luther Barr.

"That's what," assented Hank Higgins, as a tongue of flame shot upward above the black huddle of shadows that marked the town.

"I only hope it destroys their aeroplane," viciously remarked Fred Reade, "we've got to win this race."

"I suppose you've been betting on it," sneered old Barr.

"And if I have it's none of your business, is it?" demanded Reade fiercely.

"Oh, no; not at all. Don't be so savage, my dear young man, or I shall have to ask Hank here to subdue you," smirked old Barr.

"He'd better not, or I'd soon fix him with this."

Reade drew out a huge revolver and brandished it, at which the desperado grinned despisingly.

"Why, you'd be scared to handle it, even if you knew how. You let shooting irons alone till you git through with your nursing bottle," he sneered.

"I've a good mind to show you," shouted Reade angrily.

Old Barr quieted him with a reassuring tap on the shoulder.

"My dear young man, you are of undoubted courage. I believe you would fight a regiment if you thought it necessary."

Like all cowards, Fred Reade was very susceptible to flattery.

"You have the right estimation of my character, Mr. Barr," he blustered; "this wild and woolly westerner here cannot appreciate a man of grit and brawn unless he wears a pair of moustaches like a billygoat and swaggers around drinking at frontier bars."

"Is that so, Mister Reade?" sneered Hank Higgins, despite Barr's urging him to keep quiet. "You're a writing gent, ain't yer?"

"I am a journalist—yes, sir."

"Wall, while we are waitin' here and watching that ther pretty bonfire that Noggy Wilkes and our Wild friend have lit up, I'll just tell you a little story of one of your trade who come out west looking for sensations."

"All right, go ahead and amuse yourself," said Reade sullenly.

"Don't get mad."

"Oh, I'm not mad. But cut out all your talk and tell your story."

"Very well, Mr. Reade, it goes this way. One night there was seated in the bar at El Paso a young writing gent just like you are. He was a very bored young writing gent, and he says to a fren' who was with him:

"'I thought the west was full of sensations. It's deadly dull as I find it. Why don't suthen happen?'

"Wall, partner, jus' then two gents as had bin ridin' cattle for a considerable period, an' hed quite a hatful of coin ter celebrate with, blew in.

"'Ho! see that little feller!' says one, indercating the tenderfoot writing chap. 'I'll bet he's a good dancer.'

"'I'll bet he is, too,' says the other. 'Kin you dance, stranger?'

"'No,' says the tenderfoot, 'I can't.'

"'Oh, you cawnt, cawnt you,' says one of the range-ridin' gents. 'Then this is a blame good time to larn.'

"With that Mister Reade he whips out a big gun—jes like this one I've got here it was—and says:

"'Dance!'

"'I cawnt, I told yer,' says the tenderfoot.

"Bang! goes the old shooting iron, and the bullet plows up splinters right under his left foot. Wall, sir, he lifted that foot mighty lively, I kin tell yer. Livelier than a ground-owl kin dodge inter its hole.

"'Now, dance!' says the cattleman.

"'I cawnt,' says the tenderfoot, still unconvinced of the powers that lay in him.

"Bang!

"This time it come under his right foot, and he lifts that.

"'Now, do it quick,' says the range rider, and they do say that the way that feller shuffled his feet while them bullets spoiled a perfectly good floor under 'em was as purty to watch as a stage show. Wall, later in the evening them two cattle rustlers gits tired of that an' they gits in a game of poker. Now, there's where that tenderfoot should have quit, but he didn't. He goes and sits inter it with 'em. Wall, purty soon a dispute arises. One of them cow-punchers calls on the other to lay down his hand, and there, stranger, they each have three aces."

"Wall, you couldn't see the room for smoke, they shot so fast, and one of 'em died there and other on the doorsill. Wall, there had ter be an inquest, yer know, and among ther witnesses they rounded up was this yar tenderfoot."

"'Whar was yer when ther first shot was fired?' the coroner asks him."

"'At the poker table,' says the tenderfoot."

"'And when the last was fired?' goed on the coroner."

"'At the Southern Pacific depot,' says the tenderfoot, and I reckon that's the kind of a gun fighter you are, young Mister Reade," he concluded.

By the time Hank Higgins concluded his narrative the glare of the fire had spread over the whole sky, and the sounds of excitement in the town could be clearly heard. Perhaps this was what prevented the men in the waiting auto hearing the approach of another car till it was close upon them. At any rate, the other auto, which did not have any lights, was close up to them before Luther Barr exclaimed triumphantly:

"Good; they got it."

"Is the aeroplane destroyed?" was the first question Reade asked.

"Did you get the man?" was Luther Barr's eager query.

"One at a time, one at a time," growled Wild Bill Jenkins, "we've had enough trouble to-night without answering a dozen questions at once, ain't we, Noggy?"

"That's right," grumbled Noggy Wilkes, who was driving the auto, "and I'm none too skillful now at driving a buzz wagon, although once I owned one."

"Well, I reckon you see that we set the fire all right," remarked Wild Bill Jenkins, "and the joke of it was we could hear the kids warning that old fool of a mayor about the attempt we were going ter make ter attack 'em all the time we was settin' the fire and putting kerosene on it."

"Ha, ha, ha," laughed Noggy Wilkes, as if an immense joke had been related.

"Now, tell us, what about the aeroplane?" demanded Reade.

Now Wild Bill Jenkins and Noggy Wilkes had agreed to make all they could out of the deal they had undertaken, so when Fred asked this in an eager voice they responded:

"Oh, she's all burned up. Nothing left of her."

"Good," exclaimed Reade, passing over a fat roll of bills, "now, we can go ahead just as slowly as we like when we get to the mine at Calabazos. If we can file the claim to it it will be worth a lot more to us than winning the race."

"Speaking of the mine," put in Luther Barr, "where have you got Witherbee?"

"Right in the tonneau, guv'ner," responded Wild Bill; "he made a lot of trouble and I had to give him a tap on the head to quiet him, but he'll come to all right."

"It's just as well," approved Luther Barr, "it will keep him quiet. Have you searched him yet?"

"No, not yet; we wanted to get out of town before those kids found out we'd swiped the auto. They can't get after us in anything faster than an old buggy, and we'll be far away by the time they pick up the trail."

"Well, as you haven't searched him, you might just as well leave him where he is till we get to the place. You know that we are not going to Pintoville."

"Not going there, guv'ner!" echoed Wild Bill amazedly.

"No, I said we were at Pintoville for a blind. You never know who may be listening. Instead of going there we will make for White Willow. We've got the aeroplane there."

"Say, guv'ner, you're a smart one."

"That's how I made my money," grinned old Luther Barr.

"Then, you've not been in Pintoville at all?"

"No, not for a minute. We had to land at White Willow; there's something gone wrong with the engine of Slade's ship. They are working on it now."

"That's why we were so anxious to have the boys' aeroplane disabled, so that we could take our own time," put in Reade. "You are quite sure it is burned up?"

"Sure; why, I saw it with these here eyes," declared Noggy Wilkes. "Do you think we'd have taken your money if it hadn't bin all destroyed, Mr. Reade?"

"What do you think we are — thieves?" demanded Wild Bill Jenkins, with what sounded like real indignation.

"Come, come, let's be getting on," urged old Barr. "They may pick up our trail, you know."

As he spoke and the autos started, there was a low growl of thunder. One of the rare thunderstorms that occasionally sweep over the desert where it adjoins the mountains was coming up.

"Not after the storm they won't," laughed Hank Higgins confidently, "the rain that that will bring will mighty soon wash out our trail."

As they speeded along a few minutes later the rain began to fall in torrents.

"Good-bye, boys, you'll never catch us now," exultingly cried Luther Barr.

A short time later they rolled into White Willow, where, on account of the size of the party, a whole house—of which there were many vacant in the half-abandoned settlement—had been engaged. As the autos drew up the downpour ceased and the growls of thunder went rolling away in the distance.

"Say, that feller's bin mighty quiet; we'd better have a look at him," suggested Frank Higgins; "maybe you tapped him too hard, Wild Bill."

"Not me," laughed the other. "I've stunned too many of 'em for that, but he fit so hard I had to wrap him up in a blanket."

"He throwed it over him so sudden I didn't even see his face," said Noggy admiringly; "he's a quick worker."

"Well, that makes no difference; I knowed him the minute I seed him," confidently declared Wild Bill; "you gave me a good description—gray whiskers, tanned skin and a gray hat. Here he is as large as life."

He drew back the blanket that had covered a figure lying in the tonneau of the big car. As he did so, Luther Barr and the others who were crowding round with a lantern gazed on the still features with a howl of rage.

"You fool," fairly shrieked Barr, springing at Wild Bill in his anger, "*that's the wrong man!*"

CHAPTER XVIII. WIRELESS.

"What is to be done?" It was Frank who spoke, and there was a note of despair in his voice.

The boys had finished breakfast with what appetite they could and were seated on the porch of the hotel discussing plans. It seemed impossible that they could get away from Gitalong, as, without the escort of the auto to carry the necessary supplies for an emergency, it would have been futile to think of navigating above the desert in an aeroplane. The dirigible, of course, could carry her own supplies.

"Wall, now, thar ain't no use givin' up hope," consoled Bart. "Why, once when I was up a tree with a b'ar at ther foot of it, I thought I'd never git away, an' what do you think happened—why, ther b'ar jes' turned up his toes and died."

Even this anecdote of Bart's pard did not cheer the boys up, however, and in a disconsolate group they walked down the street to look over the *Golden Eagle*, which still stood where she had been left. Quite a crowd was clustered about the machine, and as the boys came up a hail of questions was poured in on them.

One of the questioners, a wild-looking fellow, with long, drooping black mustache and a wide-brimmed hat, round the band of which were nailed silver dollars in a row, was particularly curious. After asking questions about every part of the machine, he started in on the wireless. Indicating the aerials he remarked:

"Say, that's a right pert little conniption, ain't it? Kin you really send messages out sky doodling through ther blessed atmosphere with it?"

"We can if we've got any one to send them to," rejoined Harry; "but I don't suppose there's any one around here who has a wireless outfit."

"Wall, now, that's jes' whar yer wrong," was the astonishing reply. "There's an old feller, I reckon he's crazy or suthin', anyhow he used ter be some sort of electrical engineer. Wall, sir, on top of his shack at White

Willow I'm blamed if he ain't got things like them wires that's strung on top of your air ship. Yes, sir, an' claims he can sind out messages, too, if thar was any one but coyotes and rattlers to git 'em."

"Whereabouts is White Willow?" asked Frank interestedly.

"Why, it's right near to Pintoville," was the answer; "a piece this side of it, I rickin."

"Pintoville," exclaimed Frank; "that's where Luther Barr said he was stopping. Say, boys, let's send out a wireless to White Willow and see if we can raise the inventor there and ascertain if our auto passed through."

"But it was late at night. They would all have been in bed," objected Billy.

"Well, it's worth trying, anyhow, so here goes." Frank sat down at the key of the *Golden Eagle's* wireless, and began tapping out "White Willow — White Willow — Willow — White Willow," till his hand ached.

"No good, I guess," he said, discouraged, as, after quite a time, no response to his call came.

"I always thought that old feller at White Willow was loco," remarked one of the crowd.

Suddenly, however, Frank held up his hand.

"He's answering," he cried.

Sure enough, over the wires came the question:

"Here's White Willow. Who wants White Willow? For five years I've been trying to get a call here, and no one ever came. Who are you?"

"We are the Boy Aviators," tapped back Frank, while the miners and cowboys gazed in awe at the blue flame ripping and crackling across its gap. "Have you seen two autos pass through White Willow?"

"They have not passed through. They are here now," was the astonishing response.

The boys saw Frank jump to his feet with an excited yell of "Hurray! We'll get them yet."

"He's gone daffy, too," exclaimed the men in the group about the aeroplane.

"Are you crazy, Frank?" seriously demanded Billy.

"The auto's in White Willow!" shouted Frank, slapping the boy on the back.

"What?"

"That's right. The old wireless man—I mean the wireless old man—no, I don't—oh, what I do mean is that we've got to get over there in jig time. Come on, Harry, climb aboard. Bart, we'll need you, too."

"What, me git in that thar thing?" dubiously responded the miner. "No, sir, I've walked like a Christian all my days on the earth, and I ain't goin' to tempt Providence by flying at this time of life."

"Hullo! hullo! what's all this?" came a deep voice, as a big man elbowed his way through the crowd. "What's all this about flying?"

"It's the sheriff," called some one.

In the meantime the big man had made his way to Frank's side as he leaned over testing the gasolene tanks and the amount of water there was in the radiator receptacle.

"Here, young feller," he exclaimed, "I don't know if it's legal to go flyin' aroun' in this county. Hav yer got a permit or suthin'?"

"No," replied Frank; "but if you are the sheriff there are some of the worst men in your jurisdiction right in White Willow now."

111

"The blue heavens, you say. Who air they, young feller?"

"Wild Bill Jenkins, Hank Higgins and Noggy Wilkes."

"Why, thar's a reward for Wild Bill Jenkins!" exclaimed the sheriff.

"Well, you can get it if you hurry over thar."

"Hold on a minute, young feller. How do I know you ain't fooling me?"

"Because I was talking to a man in White Willow a few minutes ago."

"What's that? Say, be careful how yer string me."

"I certainly was, and he told me that the men we are in search of came there in two autos last night."

"Say, stranger, the heat's gone to yer head, ain't it?"

"Not at all. You've heard of wireless?"

"Yes; but that's all a fake, ain't it?"

"If you'll jump in and ride with us to White Willow I'll soon show you how much of a fake it is," rejoined the boy.

"What! jump in that thar wind wagon? Why, boy, I've got a wife and family to look arter. If I went skyhopping aroun' in that thar loose-jointed benzine broncho I might break my precious neck."

"I'll guarantee your neck," spoke up Harry.

"Say, boys, ef thar sheriff don't want ter go, I'll go along with yer. Thar's $25,000 reward fer Wild Bill Jenkins, an' I'd jes' as soon take a chance ter git thar money. Giv me yer warrant, sheriff, an' I'll serve it fer yer and split ther reward."

The speaker was a wiry little cowboy, apparently just in off the range, for he held by the reins a small buckskin broncho.

"What's that, Squainty Bill?" bellowed the sheriff. "I allow Tom Meade ain't going ter allow the perogatives of sheriff tuk away frum him by no sawed-off bit of a sagebrush chawing, jackrabbit of a cattle rustler. Come on, boys, show me how you git aboard this yer atmospheric ambler of yourn, and we'll git after Wild Bill Jenkins."

The boys soon helped the redoubtable Tom Meade into the chassis, and while the other lads held the machine back Frank shouted for a clear road. He didn't get it till he opened up the exhaust on the engine, and they were roaring like a battery of gatling guns going into action. Then he got it in a minute. There were four runaways and five cases of heat prostration right there.

"Let go," shouted Frank.

"Hey! hold on, young feller," cried the sheriff, starting to scramble out. Harry seized him just in time, for the *Golden Eagle* shot upward like an arrow under the full power of her hundred-horse engine.

"Say, young tenderfeet, Tom Meade ain't no coward; but no more of this fer me if I ever git out of this alive," gasped the sheriff.

"Oh, you'll get used to it in a minute and enjoy it," laughed Harry. "Say, Frank, muffle those exhausts, will you? They make so much racket you can't hear yourself think."

Frank cut in on the muffler, and instantly the noise sank to the soft droning purr of the perfectly working engine.

"Wall, if this don't beat lynching horse thieves," remarked the sheriff admiringly as the aeroplane rushed through the air. He was much reassured by the absence of noise that had ensued when the muffler came into action.

"You'll have to be our guide, sheriff," said Frank suddenly. "Where do I steer for White Willow?"

"Wait a minute, young feller! I'm all flabbergasted. Ah, now I've got it— aim right for that thar dip in the Saw-buck foothills. That's it, and when you open up old Baldy between it and Bar Mountain, then you're right on a line for it."

In a few minutes Frank sighted the peaks named, and following directions, they soon saw a huddle of huts dumped down on the prairie a short distance from them.

"That's White Willow," said the sheriff.

"But there isn't a tree round it, white or any other color," objected Harry.

"I reckon that's why they called it White Willow," was the rejoinder, "so as folks lookin' fer shade could take the mental treatment."

As they neared the little settlement, beyond which lay some rugged foothills honeycombed with old mine shafts, the boys saw an automobile full of men dash out of the place and speed off westward across the plain.

"There they go!" shouted the sheriff. "Consarn 'em, they've given us the slip."

"Not this time!" exclaimed Frank, as the auto came to a sudden stop.

Something had evidently gone wrong with it.

CHAPTER XIX. ARRESTED BY AEROPLANE.

What had happened soon transpired as the men in the auto hastily jumped out and started to rip off the shoe of a rear tire.

"I guess a cactus thorn punctured them," commented Harry.

"That's just about what happened," rejoined Frank.

"I see Wild Bill Jenkins," suddenly shouted the sheriff. He bent over and picked up one of the rifles with which the side of the chassis was furnished.

A hasty exclamation from Frank checked him.

"Don't shoot!" cried the boy

"Wall, stranger, if you don't beat all. The reward holds good for him alive or dead."

"Well, we can just as easily capture him alive," said Frank coolly, "and I don't want to see human life taken in that wanton manner."

The sheriff regarded him amazedly, but nevertheless put down the weapon.

"Wall, if we lose him it will be your fault," he remarked grimly.

But they were not to lose the desperado. As the aeroplane swooped to earth the sheriff hailed the auto party which comprised Luther Barr, the red-bearded man, Wild Bill Jenkins, and Fred Reade. They looked up from their frenzied efforts at adjusting the tire and, surmising from the authoritative tones of the sheriff who he must be, old Barr hailed him in a piping voice:

"We have done nothing against the law, sheriff. What do you want?"

By this time the aeroplane had come to a standstill, and the boys and their companion were on the ground.

"I ain't so sure about that frum what these boys told me of yer doings last night," said the sheriff dryly; "but as they ain't got no proof on you, I suppose we can't arrest yer. But we want one of your party—Wild Bill Jenkins yonder."

As he spoke there was the vicious crack of a pistol, and the sheriff's hat flew off. The man they were in search of had hidden himself behind the tonneau of the machine, and it was he who fired the shot. There would have been further shooting but for the fact that at that moment old man Barr, much alarmed lest he should be implicated in the proceedings, called out:

"You had better give yourself up, Bill Jenkins. I won't protect you."

"That's because I didn't kidnap the right man for you, you old scalliwag, I suppose, and you got my plan of the mine, too," angrily muttered Wild Bill. "Well, I'll get even with you yet. All right, sheriff, I'll go along with you."

"Just stick up those hands of yours first, Bill, and throw that gun on the ground," ordered the sheriff.

The bad man, realizing that there would be no use in putting up a fight, meekly surrendered, and a few seconds later he was handcuffed.

"Now, then," demanded Frank, stepping up to Luther Barr, "where is our auto that you stole last night and where is Mr. Joyce?"

"Your auto that *we* stole, my dear young man?" meekly inquired Barr.

"Ha! ha! ha! that's a good one," laughed Reade.

"Yes, that you stole—you or the ruffians you have chosen to make your associates."

"I don't know anything about that," resumed old Barr; "but I will tell you this: two bad men, named Hank Higgins and Noggy Wilkes, *did* bring an auto in White Willow this morning. I suspected they'd stolen it somewhere."

"Ha!" cried the sheriff, "I want those fellows, too. Where are they?"

"How do I know, my good man?" asked Luther Barr.

"Well, if you won't tell, I've got no means of making you," rejoined the sheriff, "although I'm pretty sure you do know. By the way the boys told me your party had two autos. Where's the other?"

"Why—why, it's gone on ahead," said old Barr, who seemed somewhat taken aback.

"Gone on ahead? Then, that's where Hank Higgins and Noggy Wilkes are, for sure," exclaimed the sheriff. "Well, it's no good chasing after them now, besides, there's no reward for them, anyhow."

"At least, you will not be so hard-hearted as not to tell us what has become of Mr. Joyce?" said Frank, seeing that it was no use to threaten old Barr, who seemed to have the upper hand just then.

"Joyce—Joyce," repeated Barr, professing to be very much puzzled. "Oh, yes, I do remember an old man of that name—one of your friends, wasn't he? Why, my dear boys, if you don't know where he is how should I?"

"Base as you have shown yourself to be, I didn't think you would carry your wickedness to this pitch," exclaimed Frank, his fingers itching to strike Reade, who sat by with a sneering smile on his face while his aged companion mocked the boys.

"Come, Harry, there is no good waiting here," he went on. "We must get back to White Willow. Mr. Joyce must be there. But, mind," he exclaimed, "if any harm has come to Mr. Joyce I shall hold you responsible before the law for it."

Still sneering, Barr and his companions drove off.

The sheriff accepted the boys' offer to carry them through the air back to White Willow, and in a few minutes' time they were there, Wild Bill Jenkins, it is safe to say, being thus the first prisoner to be carried to jail in an aeroplane. The first man they sought out in the town was the old inventor to whom they had sent the wireless message. They found him a dreamy, white-haired man, more interested in his inventions and their aeroplane than in the questions with which they plied him. He insisted, in fact, on taking them up the hillside, in which scores of abandoned mine shafts still remained, to show them an invention he had for washing gold. He was in the middle of exhibiting the workings of his device when the boys were startled to hear a low groan which seemed to come from near at hand.

At first they had some difficulty in tracing it, but they finally located the sound as proceeding from the mouth of one of the empty shafts.

"Who is there?" they shouted, while the old inventor stood in amazement.

"It must be the ghost of Bud Stone who fell down that shaft and was killed," he exclaimed and started to run away.

"Who is there?" cried Frank again, leaning over the deep pit which seemed to be of considerable depth.

"I am Eben Joyce—help me!" came a feeble cry from the regions below.

"Hold on!" shouted Frank. "Be brave, and we'll soon have you out. Are you hurt?"

"No; but I am most dead from thirst," came the answer.

"Have you strength enough to attach a rope beneath your shoulders if we lower one to you?"

"Yes—oh, yes. Oh, boys, please get me out of this terrible place."

It did not take long to get a rope and followed by half the population of the little town, the boys made their way back to the mouth of the shaft. But here a fresh difficulty presented itself. It seemed that old Mr. Joyce had swooned. At all events he did not answer their shouts to him.

Frank began making a noose in the rope which he slipped under his own armpits.

"What are you going to do?" asked Harry.

"Going down there to get the old man out," was the cool reply.

Despite Harry's protestations Frank was finally lowered over the lip of the black pit. It had been agreed that after he reached the bottom that two tugs was to be the signal that he wished to be hauled up. Pretty soon the men lowering him felt the rope slacken and knew that he had reached the bottom of the pit. It seemed a long time before the reassuring two tugs gave them word that all was well.

But when they started to haul the boy and his unconscious burden up a fresh difficulty presented itself. The rope which was already badly chafed would certainly break under the uneven hauling of the men, and also the rough edge of the pit mouth would undoubtedly wear it through before the boy and the old man had been hauled to the surface.

"Get another rope," cried Harry.

"There ain't another long enough in the camp, stranger," replied one of the army of rescuers.

"Here, I hev it," suddenly exclaimed the sheriff, who, by this time, had placed his prisoner in the town lockup and had joined the onlookers, "let's git a log of wood and use it as a roller."

"That's a good idee," was the consensus of opinion, and soon two men were lying one at each end of a round log, over which the rope had been run. Then the crowd began to heave again, but although their intentions were good their manner of hauling was so jerky that every tug strained the rope almost to breaking point.

"Ef only we had a windlass," groaned the sheriff, "we could git a good, even pull and soon hev 'em on terrible firma."

"I know what we can do!" suddenly exclaimed Harry, "we can hitch the rope to the automobile and get them out."

In his excitement he had forgotten that they had not yet located the auto.

"But where is yer buzz wagon?" objected the sheriff.

"That's so," said Harry in a chagrined tone. "Where can they have hidden it? It must be here somewhere."

"What's that, young feller?" asked a tall man in blue overalls.

"Why, our auto. Some men stole it last night and drove it here. They stole the poor old man who is down in the pit, and brought him here in it," exclaimed the excited lad. "So far as we know, it's here yet, but we don't know whereabouts."

"Maybe I kin help yer, thin. There's a buzz wagon down back of my house behind a haystack. Looks like some one tried to hide it there."

"That's it," cried Harry, racing off and in a few minutes he was back with the auto which, to his great joy, was found to be unharmed.

To attach the rope to it was the work of a second, and then as Harry started up the engine the half-suffocated man and boy were hauled out of the pit. It took quite a little time for old man Joyce to recover, but Frank was soon himself again. As soon as he could talk Mr. Joyce told the boys that in their rage and fury at finding that he was the wrong man and not Bart Witherbee whom they had intended to kidnap, Barr and his associates had lowered him into the mine shaft, and then on the threat of shooting down it and killing him, had made him undo the rope, which they then hauled up.

"I wonder what became of Barr's other auto?" queried Frank as the boys and their friend, the sheriff, surrounded by an admiring crowd, walked back toward the town.

"Why, Barr said it had gone on ahead," replied Frank. "Maybe he wasn't telling the truth, though, and it's still here."

But the other auto had gone on ahead, as the boys found out later, and in it had also gone the Slade aeroplane, repairs on which had not been finished. But White Willow, having suddenly come to be regarded by Luther Barr, for obvious reasons, as unhealthy, it had been decided to hustle the machine out of town on the motor car.

"But," exclaimed Harry, when the boys heard of this from some men in the town who had seen the aeroplane loaded onto the automobile, "that is an infraction of the rules of the race. The contestants must proceed under their own power."

"Well, we'd have a hard time proving they did such a thing," rejoined Frank, "so the best thing for us to do is to buckle down and make up for lost time. We'd better get right over to Gitalong in the auto, pick up the others, and start on our way. You can drive over with Mr. Joyce, and I'll fly the *Golden Eagle* over."

The rejoicings in Gitalong on the part of the young adventurers may be imagined when they saw the auto coming, speeding over the level rolling plain with the aeroplane flying high above it. The sheriff and his prisoner followed on horseback. With warm handshakings and amid a tornado of cheers and revolver shots, the boys started off once more on their way half an hour later, more determined than ever to win the great prize.

CHAPTER XX. CAUGHT IN A STAMPEDE.

That night, as may be imagined, the adventurers spent in hearty sleep. Although they had no means of knowing how far behind they were in the race, at the same time they were too exhausted by the exciting events through which they had passed to consider anything except refreshing their wornout frames. But boy nature is a wonderful thing, and both Mr. Joyce and Bart Witherbee were hard as nails, so when the entire party awoke the next day — well over the border line into Arizona — they were as refreshed as if they had rested a week.

Breakfast was over, the auto packed and everything ready for a start when suddenly in the distance a low growling was heard, something like the voice of an approaching thunderstorm.

"Thunder!" exclaimed Billy; "if that isn't tough luck."

"Thunder!" echoed Bart incredulously; "not much. Why, the sky's as clear as a mirror."

"Well, it's queer, certainly," agreed the others, looking about, but as they saw no cause for the queer noise the auto party got aboard and Frank and Harry mounted in the aeroplane.

The desert in this part of Arizona is full of little dips and rises, and from the dip on a river bank where grew a sparse collection of trees, by which the boys had camped, they had not been able to see far across the plain. As soon as Frank and Harry rose in the air, however, they perceived at once what had been the cause of the rumbling sound they had heard.

Not more than a mile away, and coming toward them like the wind, was one of the deadliest perils of the plains.

They shouted warnings to the boys in the auto below.

"What's the matter?" yelled back Lathrop, who was at the wheel.

"Matter?" shouted back Frank. "There's a herd of stampeded cattle coming straight for you."

The effect of these words on Bart Witherbee was electrical.

"Great guns, boys!" he exclaimed; "that's the worst news we could have. If we can't escape them we are as good as dead. Put on all the speed you can."

Only half realizing the terrible nature of the peril so rapidly approaching, Lathrop put on all the speed the auto possessed, and the machine seemed to fairly leap forward. Bart Witherbee stood up in the tonneau the better to see what was approaching behind them. Even he blanched under his tanned, weather-beaten skin as he saw that the cattle, an immense herd, were advancing in a crescent-shaped formation that seemed to make escape impossible.

Billy Barnes, who stood at his elbow, also sighted the maddened steers at the same moment as they rushed over a rise not more than half a mile away now.

"Whatever started them?" he gasped.

"Who can tell, lad, a coyote jumping up suddenly, the hoot of a ground owl, anything will start cattle stampeding when they are in the mood for it."

The herd came swooping on, but so far the auto, which seemed to be fairly flying over the ground, maintained its lead. The steers were bellowing and throwing their heads high in the air as they advanced, and the noise of their hoofs seemed a perfect Niagara of sound.

"Get your gun out and load. We may have to use 'em before long," exclaimed Bart Witherbee. "Sometimes the noise of shooting will turn a lot of stampeders."

"Do you think it will stop them?" asked Billy.

"I dunno," was the grim reply. "Maybe yes, maybe no. We've got to try to save our lives as best we can."

On and on went the chase, the auto fleeing like a scared live thing before the pursuing peril. Bart Witherbee's face grew grim.

"Won't they get tired soon?" asked Billy, who couldn't see how the steers could keep up the terrible pace much longer.

"Tired," echoed the plainsman, "not much, lad. It'll take a whole lot to tire them. Why, I've seen 'em go clear over a cliff. They're like mad things when once they're stampeded."

Suddenly the auto came to a stop.

Suddenly the auto came to a stop.

"What's the matter?" shouted Witherbee, in a sharp tone that showed his anxiety.

For reply Lathrop pointed ahead.

Right in front of them was a deep arroyo or water course with steep banks fully thirty feet in height, effectually blocking progress. The boys were trapped.

"What shall we do?" cried Lathrop with a white face.

"Not much of anything as I can see," replied Bart with a shrug. "Looks like this is our finish."

On swept the steers. The boys could now see the angry little red eyes of the leaders gleaming savagely. Their horns were as long and sharp pointed as spears.

"Everybody get out your guns and fire, it may scare 'em," commanded Witherbee.

Quickly the four revolvers of the party were emptied in the face of the advancing onrush, but not a steer wavered.

"It's all over," groaned Witherbee.

But suddenly a dark shadow swept down from the skies so close to the boys in the auto that they could almost feel the rush of wind as the great body swept by.

It was the *Golden Eagle*.

Frank, who, with Harry, had watched in terrible apprehension the advance of the steers, had suddenly recollected what the cowboys had said about aeroplanes scaring them. Instantly he had set his descending levers and swept in a long, low circle full in the faces of the amazed bovines.

With bellows of terror they turned, wavered and a minute later were in full retreat. They thundered past the auto in a long line, their warm breath almost fanning the occupants' faces, but none of them came any closer. Wild terror of the mysterious thing of the sky had seized them, and they were off in the opposite direction as swiftly as they had thundered in pursuit of the auto.

"Phew! that was as narrow an escape as ever I want to have," exclaimed Billy, his face still white as the last of the herd scampered by.

"Same here," echoed Lathrop.

As for Mr. Joyce and Bart Witherbee they did not say much, perhaps because they realized even more than the boys the terrible death from which Frank's bold swoop had saved them.

Looking up to where the *Golden Eagle* was soaring far above them the party in the auto set up a cheer to which Frank answered with a wave of the hand. The next instant he pointed to the westward, and—skirting the banks of the steep arroyo till they found a place where a ford had been made—the boys in the auto followed them.

Late that afternoon the character of the country over which they had been traveling began to change. The road grew rugged and in places great trees grew right up to the edge of the track and overshadowed it. The aeroplane soared far above the treetops, however, and the boys had no difficulty in keeping track of it. Suddenly, however, as they drove along the rough track, Billy, who was driving, stopped the car with a jerk.

"We can't get any further," he remarked.

"Why not?" demanded Bart Witherbee.

"Look there."

The boy pointed ahead a few feet up the road.

A huge tree lay across it, effectually blocking all progress.

CHAPTER XXI. BART AND THE B'AR.

"Well, boys, we sure do seem to be in for a run of hard luck," remarked Bart Witherbee as he climbed out of the auto with the others, and they ruefully surveyed the obstruction. It was a big sugar pine and lay entirely across the road. To go round it was out of the question, for the ground on each side was timber grown and rocky.

"There's only one thing to do—cut it away," pronounced Bart Witherbee, starting back for the tonneau to get the axes.

"No; I've got a better scheme than that," said Billy suddenly, and then broke out with a loud: "Look here, fellows!"

He pointed excitedly to the trunk of the tree where it had been severed from the roots.

The fresh marks of an axe were upon it.

"It's Luther Barr and his crowd," cried the boy. "They figured on blocking us, and they would have succeeded but for a scheme I've just thought of."

"What's that?" demanded Bart Witherbee.

"Why, let's get the rope out of the tonneau and haul the tree out of the way with the auto."

"Say, that's a good plan," assented Bart Witherbee, starting back for the auto once more. In a few minutes he had the rope and it was quickly looped round the tree and then tied to the rear axle of the auto, after the machine had been turned round.

Billy took his place at the wheel and started the car up. There was a great sound of cracking and straining, and for a second the auto's wheels spun uselessly around. Then suddenly as the boy applied more power the great log started.

Amid a cheer from the boys it was pulled entirely away, and a few seconds later the road was clear.

"Well, what do you think of men who would descend to a mean trick like that," demanded Bill angrily as the adventurers resumed the road.

"As it happened it didn't do them much good," remarked Bart.

"I should say not," rejoined Billy. "I reckon they didn't think that we could hit upon a way of getting it off our track."

The auto chugged on through the sweet-smelling pine woods till the declining sun began to tint their dark branches with gold.

"Hadn't we better send the boys a wireless?" asked Billy, and as the others agreed that it was important to know where they were the mast was set in position and a call sent out. A reply was soon obtained from the others, who were camped at a small plateau further up the side of the foothill.

Half an hour later the boys were all in camp together, and the events of the day were discussed with much interest. It was a wild country in which they found themselves. Great stretches of barrens mingled with dense pine woods, and Frank and Harry had serious thoughts of once more taking to the plains. Bart Witherbee, however, assured them that if they kept on to Calabazos they would find a good landing and ascending place, and from there could easily wing their way to level ground. He represented to them that they would be taking a short cut also by following this route. So the boys decided to keep on to Calabazos with the old miner, a decision which was not wholly disinterested, for they were anxious to see the mine of which he had told them so much.

Naturally, the position of the other contestants in the race was a topic that came up for a lot of discussion, but the boys were still talking it over when it was time to turn in without having arrived at any definite conclusion. From what they had heard in White Willow they were pretty certain that Slade's aeroplane was disabled. Concerning the condition of the dirigible or her whereabouts, however, there was by no means the same amount of assurance.

They were chatting thus and speculating on their chance of winning the big prize when Bart Witherbee suddenly held up a warning hand.

"Hark!" he exclaimed. They all listened.

"Did you hear anything?" he asked of Frank.

"Not a thing," replied the boy.

"I thought I heard footsteps up the trail," returned the old miner, "but I guess I was mistaken."

"Why, who could it be?" asked Billy.

"It might very easily be some of Luther Barr's gang prowling about. We are near the mine now, and they are no doubt determined to get the papers showing its location before I have a chance to file my claim," put in Bart Witherbee.

The boys kept a sharp lookout after this, but they heard no more, if, indeed, there had been any sound, which they began to doubt, and soon after they were snug asleep in their blankets.

Suddenly Frank was awakened by shots and loud shouts. Springing up from his blankets he was amazed to see Bart Witherbee rolling over and over on the ground with somebody who seemed of immense size gripping him tightly.

The boy could hear Bart gasping for breath. He seemed as if he were being crushed.

Frank's shouts awakened the others.

"Robbers!" cried Billy.

"Indians!" yelled Harry.

"Murderers!" cried old Mr. Joyce, as their sleepy eyes took in the struggle.

Harry raised his rifle to fire at Bart's antagonist, whoever he might be, and was about to pull the trigger, even at the risk of hitting the miner, when Frank interrupted him with a cry of:

"Don't shoot, you might hit Bart."

"But the robber will kill him."

"It's not a robber at all," suddenly cried Frank, as the two contestants rolled over nearer to the firelight. "It's a big bear!"

"Give me a knife—quick!" gasped Bart, as he and the bear rolled about. Hastily Frank threw toward him a big hunting weapon. One of the hunter's arms was free, and he reached out and grabbed the weapon. With a rapid thrust he drove it into the bear's eye. With a howl of pain the animal raised its paws to caress its injury. At the same instant Frank's rifle cracked and the animal rolled over, seemingly dead.

"Are you hurt?" asked the boys, rushing forward to Bart.

"No, I don't think so," cautiously replied the miner, feeling his ribs. "I feel as if that thar critter had caved me in, though."

An examination soon showed that Bart was uninjured and the bear quite dead.

"That was a close call," remarked the miner, wiping his knife. "I guess that must have been what I heard prowling around here early in the evening, although that dead brute there was no more dangerous than that old sharp, Luther Barr."

"Did you think it was some of his gang attacking you?" asked Billy.

"I sure did," replied the miner. "I was lying nice and quietly asleep when all of a sudden I felt something nosing me, and could feel its warm breath on the back of my neck. If I had not been so sleepy, I'd have known it was a b'ar by the strong smell of its fur, but as it was, I thought it was Hank Higgins or Noggy Wilkes. I soon found out my mistake, though."

After this interruption the boys turned in and slept quite soundly till daybreak, when they were up and the journey to Calabazos resumed, after the bear had been skinned and the steaks enjoyed. Before the start was made Bart gave the boys full instructions for landing the *Golden Eagle* in Calabazos, which lay across a small canyon not very many miles ahead.

The road now began to dip down hill, and the auto rattled along at a lively clip. Here and there the boys noticed small huts, and tunnels drilled in the hillside, which the miner told them were abandoned claims.

"Some of them is worked yet by Chinamen," he explained: "but when the poor yellow men do unexpectedly make a strike there's always some mean cuss ready to come along and take it all away from them. I think the gov'ment ought ter do something about it.

"Half a mile ahead now is the bridge across the canyon, and then we've only got a short distance to go before we're in Calabazos. My mine is about ten miles from there," he said a few minutes later. "I wonder who is sheriff there now. You see, that makes a whole lot of difference when yer are filing a claim against a rival. You've got to have the sheriff on your side, for he can make a lot of trouble for you in getting to the gov'ment office, where first come, first served is the rule."

"But you have your claim staked, have you not?" asked Billy.

"Sure; but that don't bind it till you've registered your claim," rejoined the miner. "You see, mine's an abandoned claim, too. Old fellow name of Fogg had it once. At least I found his name cut on a tree."

And now they came to a sharp turn in the road.

"The bridge is right around the corner," said the miner, "you had better put on your brakes, Billy, or we may have a runaway, for there's a terrible steep bit of hill runs right down to it."

The boy obeyed, and it was well he did so, for while they were speeding toward the bridge, a rude affair of pine trunks laid across long stringers suspended high in the air above a pine-clad canyon, there was a sudden shout from Bart Witherbee, who was acting as lookout.

"Hold up, boy! Stop the car!" he shouted.

"What's up?" asked Billy, shutting down his emergency brakes with a snap in obedience to the miner's urgent tone.

"Look there!" The miner pointed ahead.

At first the boys could see nothing the matter with the bridge, but a second glance showed them that something very serious indeed had occurred to it.

Somebody had removed two of the trunks that formed a roadway, and right in the centre of the structure was a gaping hole. Had the auto come upon it unexpectedly it must have gone through into the depths of the canyon beneath.

They all got out of the auto, all, that is, but Mr. Joyce, who was busy figuring on an invention, and hastened down to the bridge. The planks, there was no doubt, had been deliberately removed by some one, and that those persons were Luther Barr and his party none in the party could for a moment doubt.

Suddenly the bell of the wireless on board the auto began to ring.

"The boys are sending us a message," exclaimed Billy.

He and Lathrop raced back up the hill to the car, where the latter placed the detector over his ears and tapped out his "ready" signal.

The others watched him eagerly. It was not a minute before they saw that something serious was the matter. The boy's face paled, and he seemed much concerned.

"What is the matter?" anxiously asked Bart Witherbee. "Air the boys in trouble?"

"The worst kind of trouble, I am afraid," breathed Lathrop in a tone of deep concern. "They are in the hands of Luther Barr."

"Where?"

"On the other side of the canyon."

CHAPTER XXII. AN AUTO LEAP FOR LIFE.

What was to be done?

The bridge across the canyon was impassable for an auto—that seemed certain. While the open space caused by the removal of the two planks or rough trunks was not more than four feet, still it was a distance sufficient to make anyone despair of ever getting a vehicle across it.

"We can cut some trees and split off planks?" suggested Mr. Joyce.

"That would take too long," declared the boys. "Frank and Harry need us in a hurry or they would not have sent such an imperative message. We have got to cross the canyon."

Suddenly Lathrop, who had been studying the situation, the steep-sided canyon, the roaring river on its rocky bed below the structure of the bridge itself, uttered an exclamation.

"I think I can see a way to get across that gap," he cried.

"Climb across on the stringpiece, I suppose?" replied Bart sarcastically. "I thought of that some time ago; we can easily do that, but we've got to have the auto. It's got all the supplies in it."

"No, my plan is to go across, auto and all," rejoined Lathrop.

"What! Take the auto across that gap?"

"Yes."

"Say, this is no time for fooling, Lathrop," remonstrated Billy Barnes.

"I'm not fooling. I mean it. Did you ever go to the circus?"

"Well, of all the fool questions. Yes, I've been to the circus, but what has that got to do with this situation?"

"A whole lot."

"For instance?"

"Well, you've seen an act there called 'leaping the gap' or some such name?"

"Yes, where a woman in an auto comes down a steep incline and jumps a big gap at the bottom?"

"That's it."

"But, in the circus the auto is given an upward impetus by the fact that the incline down which it runs down is curved upward at the end," objected Billy.

"So it is in this case," was the calm reply. "I've been looking it over, and it seems to me that conditions are about the same."

"As how?"

"Well, here we have a steep incline—the hill yonder," Billy Barnes nodded, "and there yonder is the gap where Luther Barr and his gang took out the boards."

"But you haven't got the upward curve at the end of your incline to throw the auto into the air and carry it safely across the gap," objected Billy.

"Oh, yes, that's there, too," was the calm reply; "do you notice that the bridge sags in the centre?"

"Yes, it does, that's true," pronounced Billy, after a prolonged scrutiny.

"Well, the boards have been taken out some feet toward the opposite side of the sag, haven't they?"

"Hum—yes, that's so."

"Well, then, there's your upward curve before you come to the gap."

"Jiminy cricket, Lathrop, you are right. Now, what's your plan—to leap the gap?"

"Yes, but we must lighten the auto. We all have cool heads, and we can stand on the edge of the gap and throw most of the heavy things in the car across the space. Then we can pick them up on the other side. That is, if we get the auto over."

Even Bart Witherbee had to agree that the plan looked feasible. All of the party, with the exception of old Mr. Joyce, had seen the same feat performed in a circus. True, in the show everything was arranged and mathematically adjusted, but the conditions here, though in a rough way, were yet the same practically. There was the descent, the steep drop, the short up-curve and then the gap. The more they thought of it the more they believed it could be done.

It did not take long to transfer most of the heavy baggage to the other side of the gap, and then came Lathrop's next order—which was that the others should shin themselves across the stringpieces to the opposite side of the gap, so that the auto might not be burdened with their weights. It took a lot of persuasion to make them do it, but they finally obeyed, and Lathrop alone walked back up the trail to where the auto stood with its brakes hard set.

The boy himself would not have denied that his heart beat fast as he approached the car. In a few minutes he was to make an experiment that might result in certain and terrible death if the slightest hitch occurred.

But he thought of his chums marooned and in the hands of their enemies on the other side of the canyon and the reflection of their peril steeled him to endure his own.

The boy took a quick glance all about him.

The spot where the auto stood was about a quarter of a mile above where the bridge joined the canyon's bank. He had then, as he judged, plenty of room in which to get up a speed sufficient to carry him safely across the gap.

For a second the thought of failure flashed across his mind, but he did not dwell on it.

What he was about to do didn't bear thinking of. It was a thing to be done in hot blood or not at all.

Slowly Lathrop climbed into the auto. He felt the heavy body of the car sway on its springs as he did so, and wondered at the same instant how it would feel in case of failure to be hurtling down — down — down to the depths of the canyon with the heavy car.

As he grasped the wheel and prepared to throw off his brake, he looked ahead. From where he was starting he could see the gap in the bridge yawning blackly.

It looked much further across than he had at first anticipated.

For a minute he felt like weakening and deciding not to take what seemed a fatal chance.

The thought of Frank and Harry in the hands of Luther Barr and his gang, however, steeled him. He gritted his teeth, jammed his hat back on his head and prepared for the start.

On the opposite side of the gap he could see the white, strained faces of his friends. For one brief second he looked at all this, wondering vaguely if it was to be the last time he was to see them, and then, with a deep intake of his breath, he released the brake and threw in the engine clutch to top speed. At the same moment he advanced his spark and felt the machine leap forward on the steep incline like a creature suddenly let loose from a leash.

Down the steep grade dashed the machine, sometimes seeming to leap several feet in the air and come down with a terrific crash as it struck the ground.

"Good thing she's not more weight in her," Lathrop thought to himself as these convulsive leaps occurred.

So terrific was the speed, it was like traveling on the back of a whirlwind, if such a thing can be imagined.

"There's no stopping now," thought Lathrop, as with a brief prayer on his lips the huge machine hustled onward like a shot from a cannon. On and on it dashed.

Showers of rocks hurled upward from its wheels were blurred discs at the pace they were making.

And now the bridge and the dark gap loomed right in front of him.

Clenching his teeth tightly, the boy gripped the steering wheel till the varnish came off on his hands. He felt the machine bound forward onto the narrow span—felt it sag beneath the unaccustomed weight.

Everything grew blurred. All he thought of now was clinging to that steering wheel to the end.

His hat had flown off long ago—torn from his head by the wind generated by the awful speed.

And now the gap itself was there. Seen momentarily, dark, forbidding—a door to death.

Suddenly, just as it seemed he was about to be plunged into the depths, the boy felt the huge machine rise under him as lightly as if it had been a feather.

It shot upward like a stone impelled by a giant's fist, hesitated for a moment at the apex of its spring, and then crashed down onto the bridge.

But the gap had been crossed.

It was several hundred feet before Lathrop could control the auto, and when he did, and the others rushed up, they found a white-faced boy at the wheel, who was as nearly on the verge of a collapse as a healthy lad can be.

CHAPTER XXIII. A MYSTERY.

The supplies that had been left on the bridge were hastily loaded into the auto, and the party once more took their seats. Lathrop had by this time quite recovered, and, in reply to all the encomiums heaped on him by the others, could only reply:

"That's all right."

With Billy Barnes at the wheel the auto chugged off once more on its errand of rescue.

Suddenly, leading up a woodland track to their right, Billy Barnes spied auto tracks.

"That must be Barr and his crowd," shouted Billy, turning the auto up the track that converged from the main road at this point.

Rapidly and almost silently the auto made its way over the beds of pine needles that covered the rough roadway. With the reduced speed at which they were proceeding the approach of the machine could have been hardly audible to a strange group onto which the auto party a second later emerged.

The persons composing it consisted of Luther Barr and the men to whom Billy had referred as composing "his gang," namely, Hank Higgins, Noggy Wilkes, Fred Reade, the red-bearded aviator, and Slade. As the auto rolled up behind them so silently that none of them apparently knew of its approach, Barr was grinning triumphantly at Frank and Harry Chester, whose aeroplane stood at one side of the clearing.

"I thought we'd lure you down here by displaying a flag," he sneered. "I suppose you thought it was your own party. Well, now, you have found out your mistake."

"Our friends will soon be here in reply to our message," said Frank, "and they will not allow you to harm us."

"Oh, I suppose you think they could answer that wireless message of yours," sneered old Barr. "Well, they couldn't, because we'd fixed it so that they couldn't. Do you think I'd have let you send out a message if I thought they could have got here? I just fooled you for fun."

"What have you done with them?" demanded Frank.

"Oh, only taken a few planks out of the bridge across the canyon so that they couldn't get across. We hold the cards now, so you might as well tell us where Bart Witherbee intends to claim his mine. If you won't, we shall see that you are put somewhere where you will get over your stubbornness."

"Oh, you will, will you?" exclaimed Bart Witherbee, suddenly stepping forward. "Not yet, Mr. Barr, and now I think as we have the drop on you, you and your friends had better vamoose—git out—run along—fade away."

"What are you doing here," stammered Reade, turning round and seeing the boys in their auto, "I thought— —"

"Yes," cried Billy, "you thought you'd fixed the bridge so as we couldn't get across—well, you hadn't; so now get along and be on your way before we summon law officers and have you placed under arrest."

"Come on, let's get out," said Hank Higgins sullenly, "the kids certainly seem to have it on us this time."

Casting glances full of malevolence at the boys, but still not daring to say anything, Barr and his companions climbed into their machines and silently made off. To their satisfaction the boys saw in the tonneau of the rear machine a lot of boxes which they knew must contain sections of the dismantled Slade aeroplane. The *Despatch* party therefore had not yet been able to effect repairs, which accounted for their desperate anxiety to detain the boys at any cost.

"However, did they come to lure you down here?" asked Billy as soon as the two autos with their rascally owners had departed.

"Why, we saw a signal waving from this opening in the woods, and thought it was you showing us where there was a good landing place. We soon found out our mistake, however," answered Frank.

"Say, boys," observed Bart suddenly, after he had earnestly scanned the sky for awhile, "we'd better be getting on. I believe we are going to have one of those storms that we get up in these hills every once in a while."

"Are they very bad?" asked Billy.

"Bad!" echoed the miner, "why, boy, ef you're wearing all your own hair arter one of 'em you're lucky."

"Well, we can't fly any further to-day," announced Frank.

"Why not?" demanded the others.

"One of our rudder wires got snapped as we came down here. It was a narrow place to land in at best."

"How are we going to get the aeroplane up the trail?" demanded Bart.

"Tow it," was the quiet response.

"Tow it. How in the name of sea-sick catamounts air we goin' ter do that?" demanded Bart.

"Easy," laughed the boy; "just hitch a rope to it, attach it to the auto and it will tow right along on its wheels."

"Yes, but the wings are too wide to pass along this narrow trail," objected Bart.

"We can unbolt them and pack them in the auto. Some of us will have to walk, but that will be no great hardship for a short distance."

"Say, Frank, you're a genius. Come on, boys, git busy with them monkey wrenches and we'll be in Calabazos to-night. Then ho—for the lost mine."

As Frank had anticipated, it was not a lengthy work to detach the wings of the *Golden Eagle*, thanks to their simple construction, and soon the cavalcade was moving forward up the mountain side with the framework of the aeroplane in tow. Stripped of her planes, she looked not unlike a butterfly from which the wings have been plucked, but the boys did not mind appearances in the saving of time they effected.

"Say, Frank, though," said Billy suddenly, as they tramped along in the rear of the auto which Lathrop was driving, "isn't this breaking the rules of the flight? Are you allowed to tow your air craft?"

Frank drew a little book from his pocket.

"In cases of absolute necessity owners and fliers of contesting craft may accept a tow, provided they do not actually load their machines on railroad trains or other means of transportation," he read. "This shall be understood not to apply to circumstances other than where an aviator finds it impossible to make an ascent from his landing place."

"I guess we are within the rules all right," said Harry.

"I think so. Of course we shall have to make out a written explanation of the case," rejoined Frank, "but it would have been impossible for us to rise from that wood clump into which Luther Barr lured us."

"Say, boy, I'm afraid we're in for it," suddenly exclaimed Bart Witherbee.

"What?" asked Frank.

"Why, the storm I said was coming up. She's going to be a rip-snorter, or my name's not Bart Witherbee."

As he spoke there came a low moaning sound in the tree-tops, and the sky began to be overcast with dark storm clouds. The dust on the road, too, began to be puffed into little whirlwinds before the breath of the oncoming storm.

Presently a few great drops of rain fell, coming with heavy splashes on the dry road, and falling with resounding splashes on the planes packed on top of the auto.

"Here she comes, boys; we've got to seek shelter some place," warned the miner.

They looked about them in vain, when all at once, up the hillside to the right of the road, they became aware of a trail leading to a ruinous-looking hut that had evidently at one time been occupied by a miner.

"We'll take shelter there, boys," exclaimed Bart, pointing to it. "I'll bet the roof leaks like a sieve, but it's better than the open at that."

Hastily the boys pulled waterproof tarpaulins, provided for such a purpose, over the framework of the aeroplane and over the auto.

"There, not a drop of water will touch them, anyhow," announced Frank, as these preparations to fight the storm were concluded. "Come on, now, for the hut."

They ran up the hillside as fast as they could, for by this time the rain was coming down in a torrential downpour, and the lightning flashes were ripping the sky in every direction. The artillery of the storm rattled awe-inspiringly. Some of the thunder claps seemed to shake the very ground upon which they stood.

As they ran Bart uttered an exclamation of surprise.

"Why, boys," he cried, "this yere trail ain't so far from my mine. It's only under that next ridge there. If a man dug a tunnel he could get there dry shod."

At the time they paid no attention to Bart's words, in such haste were they to get into the hut. They were to recollect them afterward, though, and comment on their strange significance.

Billy was the first to reach the deserted hut. With a whoop he pushed in the crazy door, but the next minute he staggered back with a cry of surprise and a scared look on his face.

"There's someone in there," he cried.

CHAPTER XXIV. THE GOLDEN HERMIT.

"Some'ne in there?" echoed the others in amazed tones.

"Yes—hark!" said the lad, holding up a finger.

Sure enough, above the moaning of the storm and the roar of the rain came a sound like a faint groaning.

"Well, come on," cried Bart; "no use stopping out here in the rain just for that. Let's go in."

Reassured by his confident manner, the others crowded in. The interior of the hut, not overlight at any time, was rendered doubly gloomy by the mantle of blackness which the storm had flung over the heavens. It was not till Frank had taken out a folding lantern from his pocket and lit it with a lucifer from his folding match box that they were able to take in the details of the strange interior in which they stood. Of course, their first task was to look for the human being or animal that Billy had heard groaning.

This did not take long. The hut was not divided into rooms, and was unceiled, the rafters being right overhead. The lamp was flashed into every corner.

To the boys' amazement, the place was absolutely empty.

"I'm sure I heard somebody groaning or grumbling," said Billy. "I'm positive of it."

"Well, maybe you are right, lad," replied Bart Witherbee, "and I rather think you are, for look here!"

He pointed to a rough sort of bunk formed of a framework of lumber in one corner of the room.

"It's warm," he said, touching it with his hand, "somebody was lying asleep here when we came up the trail—that's as plain as print—and look here, too," he went on, pointing to other signs of human occupancy the boys had not noticed when first they came in.

In rapid succession, he showed them some ashes glowing in a huge open fireplace, in front of which was an ample hearthstone. There was also a rude table in one corner, on which were the remains of what had been a rude meal.

"But where has the man gone who was in here?" demanded Frank.

"Maybe out by the back door," suggested Harry.

"There isn't one," rejoined Billy, "the door in front is the only way out."

"How about the windows?"

"The two in front are the only ones."

"Well, that's queer."

"It certainly is."

"See if there are any trap doors in the floor," suggested Bart. "These old miners are queer old chaps sometimes."

But a close search of the floor did not reveal any trace of a trap door. Much puzzled by the mystery, the boys retired to bed that night prepared for any sudden alarm. A lamp was left burning, and their guns lay ready to hand. But nothing occurred to mar the monotonous drumming of the rain on the roof, and one by one they dropped off to sleep.

It was soon after midnight that Frank awakened with a strange feeling of dread.

He looked about the room, but so far as he could see at first everything was as it had been left when they went to sleep. All at once, however, his attention was attracted to the fireplace by a slight scratching sound. He gazed over toward the hearth, and to his unbounded astonishment and no small alarm he saw the hearthstone suddenly begin to swing slowly back, and, through the aperture thus created on the side nearest the room, he saw human finger tips cautiously poking about. Suddenly an entire hand was thrust through the crack.

Suddenly an entire hand was thrust through the crack.

What was coming next Frank had no idea, but with a violently beating heart he lay watching the aperture while a second hand joined the first and gave the stone a feeble shove upward. It swung back on its invisible hinges till a space of perhaps three feet yawned between it and the floor, and then a face made its appearance.

It was the face of a very old man with venerable white beard and mild, timid, blue eyes. Frank almost closed his eyes, and from under their lashes watched the old man painfully lift himself out of the tunnel into the room. Once in the room he tiptoed about among the sleepers, gazing at them earnestly to make sure they were all asleep, and then, returning to the hole beneath the hearthstone, reached down and drew out a bag that seemed to weigh considerably.

But the exertion seemed to exhaust his feeble strength, for with a groan he fell back into a rough chair, and the sack fell from his trembling hands with a crash. The sudden sound woke all the adventurers, and they sprang to their feet with their weapons in their hands.

The sight of the feeble old man, however, gasping in the chair, with his hand on his heart as if he was in mortal pain, soon convinced them that it was no dangerous enemy with whom they had to deal.

"Don't, don't hurt me," cried the old man pitiably, as the boys and their elders closed in about him. "I will tell you all, only don't hurt me. Spare a poor old man who has not long to live; let him spend his last hours in peace."

"We do not wish to hurt you," Frank assured him, "we want to aid you. Are you ill?"

"I am sick unto death. The exertion of carrying that load of ore from the mine was too much for me. I do not think I have long to live."

"Who are you?" asked Bart Witherbee gently.

"I am Jared Fogg," replied the old man, closing his eyes as though too weary to keep them open.

"Jared Fogg!" exclaimed the others in amazed tones.

"Yes; why do you seem so surprised?"

"Why, I am the man who found your lost mine," exclaimed the miner.

"What! The man who staked out his claim there!" cried the old man.

"Yes; I thought you were dead. We all did, and I started out to find your mysterious mine. As you never filed a claim to it, I thought I had a right to stake it."

"You are right; I never filed a claim to it. I did not want other miners to come to the neighborhood as soon as they found how rich it was. So I worked it all alone. As I got the good gold out I hid it all away."

"Yes; go on," said Bart Witherbee breathlessly.

"Well, I saw that some day sooner or later someone was bound to discover it if I worked openly in it, so I started constructing a tunnel. The mouth of it is under that hearthstone, and the other end emerges into the shaft of the lost mine. For many years I have used it, and no one has ever suspected that old Jared Fogg, the hermit who lived in this hut, had thousands of dollars in gold. I am rich — ha — ha — I am rich."

The old man's face became convulsed.

"But," he went on, "now that I am dying — ah, I know death when it is coming on — I have a great wish to right a wrong I did years ago. My name was not always Jared Fogg. It was once Jack Riggs. I was once a bandit and a robber and did many, many wicked things. But one weighs on my conscience more heavily than any of the others. One night we held up the Rio Bravo stage. There was fighting, and I shot the stage driver and his wife, who, when her husband fell from the box, seized the reins and attempted to drive on. With them was their child, a lad of three or four years. That disgusted me with crime. I reformed from that night. I took the lad and raised him till he was six or seven, when he was stolen from me by a wandering circus. I have never seen him since. If I could see him, now that he has grown to man's estate, and tell him that on my death bed I beg his forgiveness for my wicked deed, I would die happy. All these years I have thought of him. If I only knew where he was now."

"Would you know him again if you saw him?" Bart Witherbee's voice shook strangely, and several times during the old man's recital he had passed his hand across his brow as if striving to recollect something. Now his eye shone with a strange light, and he bent forward eagerly:

"Yes, among a thousand!"

"How?"

"By a peculiar mark on his arm, where he was shot accidentally by one of my gang in the fight following the killing of his father."

Bart rolled up his sleeve, and the old man gave a terrible cry as his eyes fell on the dark-red scar the boys had often noticed.

"Forgive— —," he cried, stumbling to his feet and stretching out his hands as if to keep from falling.

The next moment he had fallen forward with a crash.

He was dead.

CHAPTER XXV. A FIGHT FOR FORTUNE.

The sheriff of Calabazos was sitting on the stoop outside the Government Assay Office early the next day when he was startled by a loud clatter of hoofs up the mountain side. He looked up from his absorbing occupation of whittling a piece of wood, and saw coming rattling down the trail at a breakneck speed four horsemen. They were Noggy Wilkes, Hank Higgins, Fred Reade and Luther Barr.

"Hullo, Chunky," hailed the sheriff to the government clerk, who was inside the office—a rough, clap-boarded affair on which appeared a sign, which announced in white letters that it was the "GOVERNMENT ASSAY OFFICE." "Come on out here, Barton, here come them fellers that got here yesterday with that thar skyscraper thing of theirn and purty near bothered the life out of Skol Scovgen, the blacksmith, trying to git him to make a conniption of some kind for it."

The young man who languidly consented to serve Uncle Sam in the capacity of claim clerk joined him on the porch. He also gazed interestedly at the group of horsemen, who were now compelled to slow up by the steepness of the trail.

"Seem ter be in quite a hurry," he commented, picking his teeth with a quill pick that he had acquired on his last visit to what he was pleased to term civilization.

"Yep," assented the sheriff, "I reckon they've bin up stakin' out a mine or suthin'. I hear they was talking in ther hotel last night while it was rainin' so pesky hard about a lost mine and some chap named Witherbee."

"Oh, I remember that feller Witherbee," struck in the clerk. "Went east a while ago. I recollect that the gossip was that he'd made quite a piece of money on a mine or had some sort of mine hidden back in the hills thar. I heard it was the one that belonged to old Fogg, who disappeared."

"Wall, ther fellers seem to have something of ther same kind on their minds," exclaimed the sheriff, as the party, having now left the uneven trail, came clattering down the road on their wiry horses.

It could now be seen that Luther Barr, who rode in advance of the rest, carried some sort of a paper in his hand. The arrival of the cortege had attracted quite a crowd, who gathered about the Assay Office as the riders came clattering up.

"Is this the Government Assay Office?" queried Luther Barr as they drew rein and dismounted.

"Reckon so," replied the dandified clerk with a languid air.

"Oh, you reckon so, do you?" was the impatient reply. "Well, kindly bestir yourself a little. I wish to file a claim to a mine."

"Yep—Got ther papers all made out regilar?"

"Yes, here they are. We've gotten them all right and correct. I guess there'll be no trouble about that part of it, eh, Reade?"

"I guess not," answered the individual addressed, tying his horse to the hitching bar in front of the assay office.

"All right, gentlemen," at length remarked the clerk, getting to his feet, "I guess if you come inside we can fix you up."

"Say, partner," put in the sheriff, "yer don't mind my askin' you a question, do yer?"

"Not at all," beamed Luther Barr, who was in high good humor, "ask a dozen."

"Wall, is this yar mine yer goin' ter locate the 'Lost Mine' that old Jared Fogg, who disappeared, used ter own?"

"I believe it is. Why do you ask?"

"Wall, if you'll excuse my jay-bird curiosity, I'd jes like to know how in thunder you ever located it."

"That is our secret, my man," replied the eastern millionaire briskly. "All you need to know, and this gentleman here, is that we have it legally located, isn't it?"

"Beg your pardon," remarked the sheriff. "No harm done?"

"Oh, none at all," smiled Barr. "And now, I think we'll go in and make the deal final."

They entered the office with the clerk, Hank Higgins and Noggy Wilkes remaining outside.

As Barr and Reade passed into the office the former whispered to Hank Higgins.

"Now you and Wilkes do your duty. I don't anticipate any interruption, but if there is any — —"

The two western ruffians tapped the butts of their Colts knowingly.

"We'll attend to that, guv'ner," they assured him.

Silence fell on the village street after Barr and Reade had entered the office. The crowd outside stood gaping in curiosity as to what could be the business that had brought the strangers galloping in such evident haste to the assay office. The sheriff, with a side glance at Hank Higgins and Noggy Wilkes, resumed his whittling.

Suddenly the quiet was broken by the sharp chug-chug of an approaching automobile.

"Here comes a choo-choo cart," remarked the sheriff, springing to his feet and peering up the road.

"That's what it is," answered a man in the crowd, "and coming like blue blazes, too."

As he spoke, the boys' auto swept round a wooded curve and came tearing along toward the assay office. In the tonneau stood Bart Witherbee, his face strained and eager, and holding a crumpled paper in his hand. Frank was at the wheel and the other boys were beside their miner friend in the tonneau.

"Seem ter be in a hurry," drawled the sheriff, as the party swept up to the low porch, the crowd falling back to make way for them with wondering glances.

Luther Barr's lean face appeared at the dusty window of the Government Office.

"A hundred dollars if you file that claim in time," he shouted to the astonished clerk, who thought the old man had gone suddenly mad.

Bart Witherbee made a flying leap from the auto, and almost before it stopped had raced up the steps. But before he could gain the door of the assay office he found himself looking into the muzzles of two revolvers held by Hank Higgins and Noggy Wilkes.

Bart Witherbee made a flying leap from the auto.

"Don't come no further, pardner," grinned Hank. "It might be onhealthy for you."

"Here, here; what's all this?" growled the sheriff. "I don't allow no shooting in my bailiwick. Put up them guns."

"Let me get by, Hank Higgins," exclaimed Bart Witherbee angrily.

"Hey, there; what's that name you mentioned, partner?" asked the sheriff eagerly.

"Hank Higgins, and there's his partner, Noggy Wilkes," exclaimed the miner. "The third one, Bill Jenkins, is in jail."

"Wall, if here ain't a bit of Christmas luck," shouted the sheriff exultingly. "I want 'em both for a dozen crimes. Here, you; you're under arrest. Don't move or I'll fire."

But Noggy Wilkes, with a desperate leap, had gained the side of his horse that stood, western fashion, unhitched, with the reins lying on the horn of his saddle. With one bound the desperado was mounted and galloping off down the trail. The sheriff sent two bullets after him, but both missed. Hank Higgins, however, was not so fortunate. With a muttered:

"I guess you got me right, sheriff," he submitted to arrest.

In the meantime, Bart Witherbee had burst like a whirlwind into the Government office, upsetting a desk and spilling a bottle of ink over Luther Barr, who had angrily intercepted him.

"Don't file that claim to Fogg's mine," he shouted, waving his papers above his head. "I've got a prior one."

"You have—where?" gasped the astonished clerk.

"File that claim," ordered Luther Barr. "I'll report you to Washington if you don't."

"Hold your horses," replied the clerk easily, "there seems to be some sort of dispute here. Do you lay claim to the mine?" he asked, turning to Witherbee.

"I sure do," replied the miner, "and here's my claim—the last will and testament of Jared Fogg, otherwise Jack Riggs. He leaves his mine and the treasure he has secretly hoarded from it and buried under the floor of his hut to me."

"And who might you be?" asked the clerk eagerly.

"I am Bart Witherbee, and can easily prove it," replied the miner, drawing from his pocket a number of papers.

The clerk quickly perused them and also the will.

"What time did you stake the mine?" he asked, suddenly turning to Luther Barr.

"At daylight to-day," replied the millionaire. "I guess we win."

"I guess not," snapped back Witherbee. "Old man Fogg died shortly after midnight, as I can easily prove, and therefore the will became operative at that time."

"I see you know some law," remarked the clerk. "I guess, Mr. Barr, your claim is not valid."

But Barr, raging furiously, had gone.

Outside the door he saw the boys. Beside himself with rage, he shook his fist at them. His rage was too intense to permit him to speak. The sheriff and everybody in the crowd insisted on shaking hands with Bart Witherbee and hearing again and again his strange story and the details of how the will had been found hidden in the hut. At last, however, accompanied by the sheriff, whose duty it was in that rough community to look after old Fogg's, or Jack Riggs' body, the boys and their miner friend managed to tear themselves away and sped back to the hermit's hut in their auto. They found everything as they had left it, and, on tearing up the floor, according to the instructions left in the old man's will, they found that a huge pit had been dug there, which was filled to the brim with ore which the old miser had painstakingly carried through his tunnel from his mine. A rough estimate valued it at $350,000.

"How do you suppose Luther Barr ever managed to locate the mine?" asked Frank wonderingly.

"That puzzled me, too, at first," said the sheriff, "but now, since I have found that Hank Higgins and Noggy Wilkes knew Wild Bill Jenkins, it is a mystery no longer. Wild Bill boasted some time ago that he knew where the mine was, but he was forced to become a fugitive from justice before he had time to file any claim to it."

Suddenly the voice of Billy Barnes, who had wandered out onto the trail with a rifle, was borne to their ears:

"Boys! Boys! Come quick!" he cried. There was urgent entreaty in his tone.

CHAPTER XXVI. THE SAND STORM.

Rushing out in the direction of the cries, the boys found Billy struggling in the grasp of Fred Reade, Luther Barr, and Slade, while the red-headed mechanic was striking at the aeroplane with a big wrench.

"There! If we can't fly any more, no more can you," he exclaimed viciously, making a savage smash at the engine. There was a sound of splintering metal.

"Consarn 'em, they're trying to bust up our aeroplane," yelled Bart Witherbee, making a dash at the group.

As they saw the boys and their companions coming the men took to their heels, Reade alone looking back to shout out:

"Now you can't fly, either. You're out of the race."

This the boys construed to mean that the Slade aeroplane was too badly crippled to fly. And so they afterwards learned. The engine had developed a serious flaw, and one of the cylinders was cracked from top to bottom. In the part of the country in which they were it would, of course, have taken weeks to get a new engine.

"Shall we chase them?" asked Harry.

"No, it would be useless. Hark! they're in their auto now, and would be away ahead of us by the time we got after them," rejoined Frank.

The sound of an auto's exhaust rapidly growing fainter reached their ears. It was the last they saw of Luther Barr and his gang, for that night they left Calabazos and making their way to the railroad took a train east. The skeleton of Slade's unlucky aeroplane still remains in the little settlement, and greatly puzzles visitors there, some of whom think it is the framework of some extinct animal.

Billy Barnes soon told how, while shooting in the woods, he had heard an auto coming up the trail, and suspecting some mischief had hastened to the spot where the aeroplane had been left. He found his surmise correct when

Barr and his companions suddenly emerged from the woods and began their attempt to wreck the craft. Before Billy, who indignantly sprang forward, could seize the arm of the vandal with the wrench, he had been seized. Luckily he had time to cry out before they thought of stopping him, and so the aeroplane was saved from serious damage. It was found, in fact, that the blow aimed at it had done no worse harm than to splinter a spark plug, which was soon replaced.

That afternoon the boys, leaving Bart Witherbee and the sheriff to make an inventory of the dead miner's effects and to explore the tunnel, which was found to be a wonderful piece of work, the boys motored down to the settlement and sent out telegrams seeking information of the whereabouts of the dirigible. It was not till late evening that they received from Doolittle, a small town about forty miles from Calabazos, information that the big gas-lifted craft had laid up there for repairs, but was ready to start early the next day.

To the boys who had feared that the rival must have been almost in San Francisco by that time this was cheering news, and the *Golden Eagle's* planes were hurriedly readjusted, as she was put in shape for a continuation of her trip. Early the next day the start was made. Bart Witherbee was left behind at his mine, in which he had insisted on the boys, much against their will, each taking a share. Old Mr. Joyce also received a large enough portion of the general good luck to secure him from want and give him ample leisure to work out his queer inventions. The Witherbee mine—he calls it the Aeroplane—is now one of the most famous in the west.

The boys had determined to shape their course by Doolittle, as it was on their direct path westward, and they wished also to get out of the mountainous region of the foothills. As Doolittle came in sight they had an opportunity to view their rival for the first time in many days. Her big red gas bag showed like a bright crimson flower above the sober gray of the prairie town. That their rivals had sighted them was soon made evident by the fact that a flag was run up on the single staff the town possessed and the citizens wheeled out a rusty old cannon and began firing it like mad. When the boys were within a mile of the town they made ready to drop messages which, as they sailed above, they cast down. They could see the people scrambling furiously for them.

"I hope they leave enough of them to send back home," laughed Harry as they saw the wild struggle.

That day was to be a memorable one for the town of Doolittle. As the aeroplane passed above it, the faithful escorting auto not far behind, the big dirigible also was shot into the air.

Mr. McArthur from his deck waved a greeting to the boys and hailed them through a megaphone.

"Glad to see you," he hailed. "Hurray, for 'Frisco!"

All that afternoon the two ships sailed along in company, the boys' aeroplane slightly in the lead. As the sun sank lower a big bank of clouds arose toward the north and the sun glowed with a peculiar red light.

A light breeze also sprang up, but instead of being cooling it was as hot as if it had blown from an oven door.

"We're in for a storm," remarked Frank, "or I'm very much mistaken."

"What, a regular rain and wind storm?" asked Harry. "I thought they only had those in the hills in this part of the country."

"They have a worse thing than that," said Frank apprehensively, "a sand storm, and that's what may be coming."

"McArthur doesn't seem to be worrying," remarked Harry, glancing up at the dirigible, which was sailing slightly above them.

"No," said Frank, "that's a fact. Maybe I am mistaken, after all. Anyhow, we'll keep on as long as he does."

But half an hour later the boys wished they had alighted. The wind came in sharp, hot puffs from the north, and had it not been for the Joyce gyroscopic balancer they carried, the ship would have been in hard straits.

As it was, when Frank wished to make a landing he dared not risk it. The air, too, grew so thick that he could not see the earth beneath them.

Stinging particles of sand drove into their eyes, blinding them and gritting between their teeth. The wind grew stronger, and as it did so the air grew black as night with the sand with which it was impregnated.

So dark was it, in fact, that when night came and found them still in the air, unable to make a landing, there did not seem to be any perceptible difference.

The aeroplane drove rigidly before the howling wind. Her speed was terrific. Neither boy spoke after their first expressions of alarm, but devoted their entire attentions to keeping the aeroplane from capsizing.

"Keep cool, Harry," said Frank at length. "We may come out of it all right."

"Where are we being driven?" asked the other lad.

"To the south at a terrific pace, too. If the gasolene holds out we may manage to live out the storm, but I don't know where we will be driven to."

"What lies to the south of us?" asked Harry, after another long pause, during which the storm-stressed aeroplane made several sickening lurches, always recovering herself in time, however, thanks to the gyroscope.

"Why, about as desolate a country as can be imagined. Nothing but arid wastes and cactus."

"It will be a bad lookout, then, if we have to land there."

"It certainly will," was the laconic response.

On and on through the darkness drove the storm-tossed aeroplane, carrying her two young navigators into the unknown.

CHAPTER XXVII. WINNING THE PRIZE. — *Conclusion.*

It was at four o'clock in the morning by the auto clock affixed to the chassis that Frank noticed the wind begin to drop. At the same time the stinging of the sand decreased perceptibly. The storm was waning.

He awakened Harry, who had fallen into a troubled doze, and gave him the cheering news. But even if the storm had blown itself out with the coming of daylight there was not much else to cheer the boys' hearts, for as it grew lighter and the air cleared and they found themselves able to make out what was beneath them, Harry uttered an exclamation of dismay:

"Look there!" he shouted, pointing downward.

The aeroplane was traveling over a gray waste which Frank at once realized was the sea. The question was: Was it the open ocean or the Gulf of California? It did not seem possible it could be the Pacific as, even at the terrific pace they had been carried along in the preceding twelve hours, it seemed hardly possible that they could have been blown across the long peninsula of Lower California.

On either hand, they could make out, as the light grew stronger, a thin, faint line of coast, and therefore Frank's surmise was proven correct. The boys decided to make for the land on their left, as Frank had heard that the natives of the peninsula itself were little better than savages, and not overpleased to see strangers. The land to the left on the contrary must be Mexico, where they could probably find a railroad or at least the means of transportation to one.

It was afternoon when they drew near to the coast. Not far inland they could see among the barren hills, dotted here and there with cattle, a small village. It was a mere huddle of roofs, but at least it meant food and shelter, and the boys relied on being able to find a telegraph station from which they could send out a message to relieve the anxiety of the friends they knew must be extremely concerned for their safety by this time.

Suddenly as the outlines of the melancholy-looking hills grew plainer and plainer the engine, which had been working badly, gave symptoms of stopping altogether.

The boys exchanged worried looks. Beneath them was an expanse of water without a boat on its surface, and though both of them were strong swimmers, they could not dream of reaching the shore should their aeroplane plunge downward.

It was a serious situation.

Harry tinkered with the engine, and it began to run a little better for a short time, but soon began to gasp and cough, as if in mortal distress.

"What can be the matter with it?" puzzled Harry. "Everything, ignition, lubrication and all seems to be all right."

"I have it," suddenly cried Frank.

"What is it?"

"The gasolene is running out!"

Sure enough there was hardly more than a few spoonfuls of the fuel left.

"There's some alcohol in the locker. We had it for the stove. Let's try that," suggested Harry.

The alcohol was dumped into the tank and gave them a little more fuel, but the shore still looked far away.

Lower and lower sagged the aeroplane under her decreased speed, till as they reached the shore it seemed that she was hardly skimming the waves, but she bravely struggled on, and as the engine gave a final gasp and came to an abrupt stop, the *Golden Eagle* settled down on a sandy beach.

"Well, here we are," said Frank, "and none too soon."

"Now, let's go and see what sort of folks they are in that village," said Harry. "I'm famished, and my mouth is as parched as a bit of dried orange peel."

"Same here," said Frank, as the boys set out for the interior which was hidden from them by sand dunes, topped with a sort of sharp bladed grass that cut like a knife.

The village they found to be a mere collection of shacks, with pigs roaming about its streets, and skinny cattle poking their noses into the house doors. They were received hospitably enough, however, and although they could not talk Spanish, managed to make their wants understood, more especially when they showed some gold.

The wonder of the villagers knew no bounds when, after they had refreshed themselves, the boys showed them the aeroplane and pointed to the sky. The Mexicans were too polite to say so, but it was clear that they thought the boys were fabricators, though how they imagined they had landed in their village was a matter of speculation.

That night they managed to secure a cart and, having packed the *Golden Eagle*, set out for the railroad, which the Mexicans assured them was "far, far away," as a matter of fact, it was not more than sixty miles, and the next day, late in the evening, two very dusty, very ragged, very tired boys got out of the plodding ox cart at Torres, a small town on the Sonora Railroad, and almost frightened the native operator to death by their vehement demands to file messages.

"To-morrow, to-morrow," he kept saying, but the talisman of a good, big tip kept him at work.

In the meantime the auto had gone as far adrift in the sand storm as the boys, very nearly, and the state of mind of its occupants can be imagined when they found after the storm had cleared that they had traveled miles in the wrong direction and were near to Gila Bend on the Southern Pacific Railway, with no more idea as to what had become of their young companions than they had of the direction in which the aeroplane had been blown.

Telegrams were sent out broadcast by Billy and Lathrop, but no news was had of the *Golden Eagle*. Lathrop suggested sending word east of the boys' plight, but Billy overruled this.

"They may turn up all right," he said, "and if they do, we shall have alarmed their parents for nothing."

The next day, however, while Frank and Harry were plodding across Mexico in their ox cart, Billy became so anxious that he sent word to the *Planet*, asking them to notify him at once if word was heard of the boys, as he knew that they would wire the paper as soon as they landed anywhere. No word had been received by the paper, however, and it was a gloomy party that sat on the porch of the little hotel at Gila Bend that afternoon and evening. After a troubled sleep Billy emerged onto the street in the early morning and was met by a ragged station agent.

"Be your name Barnes?" he asked.

"That's me," said Billy, wondering what the man could want.

"Then I've got a message for yer. It come late last night, but I didn't want to wake yer."

"And you've been holding it all this time?" indignantly demanded Billy, guessing at once that it was news.

"Wall, yer wanted yer sleep, didn't ye?" demanded the man.

Eagerly Billy tore the envelope open. It was from Mr. Stowe.

"Great news. Boys safe. Win the prize for longest flight. Dirigible smashed in storm near Parkerville, Arizona. McArthur and crew safe. Congratulations.

Stowe."

There is little more to tell. My readers can imagine for themselves the scene when two days later the boys met at Tucson. Over a merry meal they "fought their battles o'er again," and discussed every strange adventure of their record flight a dozen times. Their parents had been notified of their safety, and were to meet them in Los Angeles.

"Well, this trip certainly has panned out," said Frank, as the subject of Bart Witherbee and his mine came up.

"And here we are, all together, safe and sound. At one time I thought we were goners sure," remarked Harry.

"*One* time!" exclaimed Billy with a laugh. "A dozen at least."

"I'd like to start out on another trip to-morrow," exclaimed Lathrop enthusiastically.

"I'd make some new inventions for it," said Mr. Joyce.

"Here, too," cried Billy. "Do you think we will have any more adventures?"

"Sure to," said Frank.

The boys did, and sooner than they expected to. As they were talking there came a rap at the door.

"Telegram from Captain Robert Hazzard for Mr. Chester," said a grinning bell boy.

"Captain Hazzard?" said Harry, puzzled.

"Oh, I remember now!" exclaimed Frank as he glanced over the message. "It's that army officer who was chasing the Indians, and who spoke about the South Pole. I suppose he got our address from the papers."

"What does he say?" demanded Billy.

"Look here," cried Frank enthusiastically. "What do you think of that?"

Milton Keynes UK
Ingram Content Group UK Ltd.
UKHW010728200923
429044UK00004B/170